He wanted to know Cameron
as a lover

The realization surprised Paul.

"I think it would make you feel better," he said, unable to keep from smiling. Feeling mischief sweep over him. "If it doesn't work the first time, we'll do it again."

Spontaneously, he kissed the tip of her nose. Then his lips drifted to her cheek, down to her mouth.

He could smell the bread toasting, but he'd lost all interest in food.

She kissed him. She felt his mouth open slightly, and so did hers. She felt the tip of his tongue caress her lips. She whispered, "Okay."

Paul let her body settle against his, touch everywhere, let her feel what was happening to him, because of her.

Dear Reader,

In Jane Austen's *Pride and Prejudice,* Caroline Bingley, in the hope of pleasing Mr. Darcy, speculates that balls would be better if there were more conversation and less dancing. But then the events wouldn't be balls, would they?

In *Love Potion #2,* Cameron McAllister faces a similar paradox. Paul Cureux—and all men—would be much more understandable if they behaved more like women. More understandable but not nearly so much like men.

It's confusing to discover that what aggravates also attracts. Any woman who has had to persuade a man to seek medical attention for an obviously dislocated finger—or shoulder or knee—gets a fascinating picture of one way in which men and women differ. And then there's that other thing—that women typically talk about their feelings and men often do not.

Cameron perceives Paul as a Peter Pan figure who will never commit. She wants him to open up, to share his deepest emotions—or so she thinks. Only when unexpected challenges force her to rely upon him does she realize why he's the man she can't stop thinking about.

Can best friends maintain enough mystery in their relationship to keep them interested and attracted over the long run? Maybe only if they are different enough.

Wishing you happy reading and all good things always.

Sincerely,

Margot Early

Love Potion #2
Margot Early

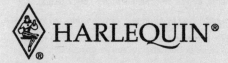

TORONTO • NEW YORK • LONDON
AMSTERDAM • PARIS • SYDNEY • HAMBURG
STOCKHOLM • ATHENS • TOKYO • MILAN • MADRID
PRAGUE • WARSAW • BUDAPEST • AUCKLAND

Recycling programs
for this product may
not exist in your area.

ISBN-13: 978-0-373-71637-1

LOVE POTION #2

www.eHarlequin.com

Printed in U.S.A.

ABOUT THE AUTHOR

Margot Early has written stories since she was twelve years old. She has sold over three million books with Harlequin Books; her work has been translated into nine languages and sold in sixteen countries. Ms. Early lives high in Colorado's San Juan Mountains with two German shepherds and several other pets, including snakes and tarantulas. She has studied herbalism and martial arts, and she enjoys the outdoors, spinning dog hair and dancing with Caldera, a tribal belly dance troupe. You can find her on Facebook.

Books by Margot Early

HARLEQUIN SUPERROMANCE

Don't miss any of our special offers. Write to us at the following address for information on our newest releases.

Harlequin Reader Service
U.S.: 3010 Walden Ave., P.O. Box 1325, Buffalo, NY 14269
Canadian: P.O. Box 609, Fort Erie, Ont. L2A 5X3

For Chris

Acknowledgments

Thanks to Chris Chambers, for reading
the manuscript and sharing birth knowledge
and valuable life experience, and to
Keiran Woodhouse and the other members of
Rhesus, for their CD which became a sort of
soundtrack for the writing of this book.

All technical errors in this fictional work
are mine.

PROLOGUE

All Saints' Day
Seven years past
Wrightsville Beach, North Carolina

TWENTY-ONE-YEAR-OLD Cameron McAllister had woken up happy. She'd woken up with Paul Cureux, her best friend from high school in Logan, West Virginia. Now, they were both students in their last year at the University of North Carolina, Wilmington. The night before had been the best Halloween of her life, partying with her three best buddies, all guys. Her costume was Love; she'd worn a toga-like garment made of an ivory bedsheet—and lots of glitter. She and Paul had ended up kissing, and it was as if she'd swallowed her breath, all the breath she would ever breathe, then exhaled, and then she was screaming down a roller-coaster hill, and then they were in bed, making love, and it was great. It was exciting. It made her wonder all the things she *didn't* know about Paul.

It had happened at exactly the right time, and now, the morning after, she was happy. Things might have become romantic between her and another friend, the Adonis-like

Sean Devlin. But Sean didn't intrigue her as Paul did—especially now.

Now, the morning after, she was happy.

Paul woke up and blinked at her, his curly dark hair mussed, and he smiled, and it was a boyish smile, straight white teeth. His brown eyes, strangely innocent; his lips full and sweetly curved; his nose classically shaped, the most perfect she'd ever seen—it was a young and beautiful face but also a comfortably familiar face.

Cameron had been in love. And off and on for the past two years, she'd considered *trying* to fall in love with her friend, Sean Devlin, who studied drama and wrote poetry and whose cheekbones could hew wood. There had been that one time, when she lost her virginity, but the chemistry just wasn't there—not on her side, anyhow.

On the other hand, last night… It had been so perfect. And Paul was her best friend. Surely, *this* was love.

PAUL CUREUX peered down at his dark blue sheets. They were now sprinkled with gold glitter, as though he'd been visited by a fairy.

But it wasn't a fairy beside him. It was Cameron McAllister, the unofficial Hottest Body of their year at Logan High School. His surfing buddy through their years at college, whom he'd decided, maybe unwisely, to sleep with.

It wasn't that Paul was averse to sex or to casual sex. It was just that he'd had one, perfectly good, version of a relationship with Cameron. Now, she would want him to tell her he loved her. She would want dates, presents, girlfriend things. Being from Logan, she might even want him to marry her. All these ideas gave Paul a sense of time closing in, of the necessity of "settling down," of graduation's too-fast approach. *Everything* was going too fast.

He drew his eyes from Cameron's high, perfect breasts. Yes, she was hot, but this was going to ruin everything. He grinned at her, knelt up in bed to peer out the window, and said, "Yes!" turning the focus at once to the waves and hoping she would follow his lead.

Cameron sat up, looking sleepy, and glanced out the window, too. She seemed dazed.

Paul said, "This was great. Really great." He made himself meet her brown eyes. "But I think it could wreck our friendship. I think we shouldn't do it again."

He could detect little change in her expression. Not even stiffening in her body. She jumped down from the high loft bed, raised above his stereo and drawers. "Sure," she said. "Can I borrow some clothes?"

Paul said, "Yeah. Of course." He watched her open his drawer, rooting for things that would be much too big for her.

She did not look at him.

He said, "Are you okay?"

"Sure," she repeated.

He knew very definitely that she wasn't, that he'd been a clod, that he couldn't undo any of it, that he had wrecked things. Tendrils of adulthood and commitment inched toward him, crept around him, and he, too, jumped down from bed, effectively casting them off.

CHAPTER ONE

Logan, West Virginia
The present

CAMERON MCALLISTER sat at a small damp table in The Last Resort, the downstairs lounge of a Stratton Street hotel, now in its fifth or sixth incarnation. She listened without much interest to Paul Cureux's final set and tried to look like his girlfriend. She felt desperately sad, help-lessly jealous and reckless.

Her first reckless act of the evening had been to attend a family birthday dinner, where the man she most desired had shown up as her cousin's date. *And* obviously mad about said cousin. Thus Cameron's desperate sadness and helpless jealousy.

The second reckless act had been to pour the contents of an innocent-looking vial into her wine glass and drink it. This was supposed to help her get *over* the man in question.

Her third reckless act had come with Paul's phone call, his insistence that one of his most infatuated fans was at his gig and not getting the message that he had a girlfriend.

This was hardly surprising; Paul didn't have a girlfriend. Paul had Cameron. Cameron, who was, she supposed, his best female friend and had been since they were thirteen. Cameron, who was willing to assume the public-only role of his girlfriend. The system worked well enough. The reasons she took part—at parties, gigs and such—were myriad and not something she ever fully examined. Paul's reasons? Well, she wasn't wholly sure about that, either, except that he didn't *want* a girlfriend and her presence prevented his ever finding one. Though he occasionally slipped away for the night with the kind of woman he believed least likely to ever trouble him again—almost always at out-of-town gigs.

Paul was the son of a midwife who brewed love potions for the occasional desperate petitioner. Love potions that he, at least, believed worked. And his sister, Bridget, claimed to have the same powers as his mother, though the little vial Cameron had bought from her (and dumped in her wine) was *not* a love potion. Paul held up his sister and mother as examples of the inherent untrustworthiness of the female sex. Because women were like this, he said, half-facetiously, he would never marry.

Nonsense, in Cameron's opinion. Paul would never marry because he was Peter Pan. He had told her many times that he didn't want so much as a houseplant; the responsibility of marriage and children was not for him.

Oh, if only Bridget's concoction to "restore emotional equilibrium" would actually work. Cameron believed in the love potions, believed them to work. But this was a different kind of potion. One that was supposed to help her get over Graham Corbett. And *that* was absolutely necessary.

Cameron's cousin Mary Anne was beautiful, talented and her best friend. Local radio host Graham Corbett was the only man who had interested Cameron in at least three years. But Graham was smitten with Mary Anne, the attraction was mutual, and Cameron just wanted to be home with her dogs and a romance novel so she could start getting over it. If anything, *anything,* could distract her from the burning jealousy she felt…

Cameron was rarely jealous. She made a habit of contentment. Someone had once told her that grateful people are happy people, and she counted her blessings daily. Decent looks, good health, two dogs she loved, her job as director of the Logan County Women's Resource Center, and so much more….

The girl sitting across from her said over the music, "So…where did you two meet?"

You two. She meant Cameron and Paul, the supposed couple. The groupie was very pretty. Her name was… Ginny? Jenny? No, Genie. Or Jeannie. She was blonde, with fairy-perfect skin, taller than Cameron and skinny like a model, with high cheekbones and a wide mouth. Paul had said this groupie was "clingy," but why should that bother Paul? What was wrong with having a gorgeous woman infatuated with you?

And there was nothing to stop women from becoming infatuated with Paul. He had a fine tenor voice and made audiences laugh by spontaneously creating songs on the spot on whatever subject they requested.

Now, Paul gazed at Cameron as he sang an original love song called "Years Ago."

"We've known each other forever," Cameron replied, trying for patience. This woman should give up on Paul. She said, "Look, if you really knew him, you wouldn't want him."

Cameron was again being reckless—not to mention sounding unlike a girlfriend—but *someone* should say something to this delusional young woman. And Cameron thought most women received too little good advice when it came to men.

"You want him," Ginny-Genie pointed out.

Not really.

Cameron looked at Paul, his dark hark hair waving appealingly, just messy enough, just long enough and no longer. Cameron cut his hair; she did this because he asked her to, claiming that he worried about his mother and sister using pieces of his hair for witchcraft. Because he didn't simply go to the barber, Cameron suspected he liked her to cut his hair. He was classically handsome, his eyes perpetually alight with mischief. He was tall, lean and broad-shouldered, nothing bulky about him. He looked like a construction worker in a television ad. Or the Marlboro Man. Or an Olympian god.

In actual fact, he was a zookeeper and moonlighting folk singer who lived a self-serving existence and believed lasting marriage did not exist. Cameron had no desire to marry him, so this didn't matter.

"Look," she said to Ginny, shouting too loudly over the song Paul was pretending to sing to her, "you're very pretty, and you seem intelligent." This might be stretching it, but undoubtedly Ginny-Genie's low self-esteem was part of the reason the girl considered Paul satisfactory. No harm in a little confidence-building. "There are good men out there who would give their eyeteeth to have a girl like you, to marry her. Men who are okay with commitment."

Ginny-Genie sipped her own margarita, and there actually did seem to be a look of intelligence—or at least calculation—in her aquamarine eyes.

Knowing she'd said too much, Cameron became intent on watching Paul tune his guitar. His hands were big, long-fingered, work-roughened. He had a bandage wrapped awkwardly around one thumb where he'd sliced it open erecting the new monkey enclosure at the zoo. He'd really needed stitches but had insisted he didn't and was now, Cameron saw with much satisfaction and little pity, paying the price.

As her eyes again skimmed the lounge, she saw a big, tall man enter the bar with Jonathan Hale, the manager of the local radio station. Cameron squinted through the darkness, and the big man seemed to gaze curiously at her. Hazel eyes, she saw, and *those cheekbones*. That full mouth.

She smiled, and he broke free from Jonathan, crossed the lounge to her table. Cameron stood up to greet her first lover, who had only grown more fantastic-looking with age. Sean Devlin.

"Cameron?" he said.

"Hi, Sean. What brings you to Logan?"

"Actually, I'm living here. I'm the new drama teacher at the high school."

Yes, the old one had died suddenly three weeks earlier.

He looked down at Ginny-Genie, and Cameron introduced her, as well, not feeling possessive.

But he seemed interested in her and asked for her phone number, which she gave him before remembering that she was supposed to be acting like Paul's girlfriend.

At the end of the song, Paul asked for requests, said he hadn't made up a song yet that night. Now standing beside Sean, the groupie raised her hand.

She was the only one.

Paul lifted his eyebrows.

"Commitment," she said.

"YOU DO NOT BELIEVE one single thing you said in that song," Cameron chided Paul on the way home, remembering the song he'd created on the spot to satisfy the groupie.

"I beg to differ. I believe commitment is a beautiful thing, and I said that. And you almost blew our cover flirting with your old flame."

"He was never a *flame*. We were first and foremost friends—not unlike you and I." And she'd made love with each of them once. But there was a certain spice and bittersweet pain to the memory of the long-ago Halloween night she'd spent with Paul. With Sean—nothing, really, though he had been her first. "Anyway," she told Paul, "you believe commitment is a beautiful thing for everyone *else.*"

"May I beg to point out that I *do* have commitment in my life? I'm committed to my job and to my music. I'm just not committed to a house on Stratton Street, a wife and three kids and a golden retriever."

He pulled up outside the cabin where she lived. Two dogs got up from the porch. Wolfie was feral and didn't let anyone, even Cameron, touch him, but he sometimes walked in and out of her house and had been known to steal her stuffed animals and bury them in the yard. Mariah was Wolfie's daughter and was as well-trained as was possible under the corrupting influence of her father, who really did look like a wolf, a black wolf with gray under his muzzle. An old guy who, after being attacked by coyotes, had been darted, castrated and stitched up by the zoo veterinarian, then released to Cameron's backyard. After that, Wolfie had decided he sort of trusted Cameron.

"Whatever," Cameron muttered, pushing open the passenger door of Paul's pickup truck, an old Toyota 4Runner with camper shell. "Thanks for the ride." She slammed the door and trod up her flagstone path, a rustic path interspersed with dirt and growing things, wilted away this time of year.

A moment later, another door slammed. Cameron glanced back. She was greeting Mariah, petting her affectionate dog, while Wolfie kept his distance, still managing to look envious, yearning yet unwilling to be touched. She said, "Hi, Wolfie," then noticed Paul coming toward her in the moonlight.

Oh.

He was coming in.

She moved toward the door. "Want some tea?"

"No grass clippings."

"I can't believe your own mother is an herbalist and you talk about nettles that way."

"It's *because* she's an herbalist. As a child, I decided that in my adult life I'd never drink anything that tasted like lawn shavings."

"You have no adult life."

He ignored the jibe. They were walking through the dark hallway and had almost reached the kitchen when he said, "You look like you've lost your best friend, and there's definitely no need. Sean Devlin has arrived, looking romantic, to sweep you off your feet. I remember him as one of the sharper crayons in the box, so your children won't be cretins."

"I will *never* have children," Cameron told him sharply, "unless I adopt."

"Ah, yes. I'd forgotten your morbid fear of pregnancy and birth." Cameron had witnessed her older sister, Beatrice, in what she described as "extreme suffering, life-threatening suffering, the screaming-for-hours kind of suffering." Cameron was convinced that no child could pass through her small hips. Paul kept to the original subject. "What's making you so miserable tonight?"

"Never mind. Don't trouble yourself about it."

"Let me guess—you *have* lost your best friend. You've lost Mary Anne to Graham Corbett."

"Very funny." She took two mugs out of the cabinet, checked that there was water in the kettle and switched on the burner.

"It's inevitable that your cousin will marry someone."

Cameron's throat knotted. Her eyes felt hot. She wasn't upset because everything was going to change with Mary Anne, that her being married would change everything. That wasn't it at all. Anyhow, Mary Anne and Graham weren't actually engaged.

Not yet.

"You okay?"

The question was far from Paul's usual joking tone.

It increased the swelling in her throat. She nodded, jaw taut.

From her Salvation Army kitchen table, where he'd pulled out a chair, Paul watched her back. His tomboy friend with her two long golden-brown braids was dressed up, for her, wearing high clogs and some kind of longish, lacy tunic-top over her jeans. She'd been at a family dinner when he'd called her and begged her to come to The Last Resort.

He'd used the groupie as an excuse, but that wasn't it. He'd known something was up with Cameron, something that had to do with Mary Anne. He also knew that Cameron, for reasons that made no sense to him, was ever so slightly envious of her cousin. *She's got cheekbones! She's tall!* Things like that. He saw no reason Cameron should envy anyone. She was the best-looking and most enjoyable woman he knew, that was certain. If there had been a Best Body category in their high school yearbook, she'd have won, hands down. All his classmates had carried fantasies about her.

Now, she sounded as if she were about to cry.

She spun away from the stove and said, "If you tell anyone what I'm going to tell you, I will never speak to you again and I'll tell that groupie that you want to marry her so she can have your babies."

Some small voice in the back of Cameron's head whispered, *Reckless...reckless...don't do it.*

She ignored the voice. She couldn't stop, now that she'd started. "I just don't see why I can't have a normal relationship with a nice man who is actually an adult—someone who knows his own psyche and doesn't project his demons onto me."

Paul squinted. "Didn't Sean Devlin beg your phone number tonight, or am I imagining that? Is this going to be another salvo in the Great Crusade for All Men to Have Therapy?"

"Forget it!" She spun away again.

Cameron, he knew, didn't actually believe all men should have therapy. But she seemed to want some kind of fantasy relationship where she and the man in her life talked about *everything,* had no secrets from each other, constantly shared every emotion. Sometimes he wanted to point out to her that, in a strictly intellectual sense, she didn't want a boyfriend, she wanted a girlfriend.

But now Paul suddenly saw, suddenly understood. She wasn't crying about her friendship with Mary Anne, and she wasn't crying about the general lack of the uninteresting kind of love relationship she thought she wanted; she was crying because she wanted Graham Corbett. The radio guy who looked like an extra on *Sex and the City.* Talk about someone totally *wrong* for tomboy Cameron. And Cameron could have virtually any guy she wanted.

Paul knew it would be a mistake to say anything. Especially anything on the subject. But he had to try.

"Graham Corbett's just *not*…" he said inarticulately, unable to say exactly what Corbett wasn't.

He thought Cameron might turn around and shout at him.

Instead, she turned to face him again, dragging her sleeve across her eyes. She said, "It doesn't matter. I'm getting over him. Bridget gave me something so I wouldn't like him."

All the hair on Paul's body stood up. Bridget, his sister, was not someone you should accept funny drinks from. She and his mother had uncanny powers which Paul, who had grown up with these females, could not pretend away. He had seen too much to be complacent on the subject. "You drank something Bridget gave you?"

"A s-s-specific—" Cameron sniffed. "For emotional healing."

Paul supposed it could be true. But he also knew that his sister was mad at him. She hadn't been watching her son beside the duck pond at the zoo. It was dangerous, and he'd told her so. Not tactfully, maybe, but come on! Nick could have fallen in and drowned while Bridget was talking meditation techniques with another mom.

Cameron moved away from the counter and picked up her purse, which she'd slung onto the table. From within she retrieved a small vial that she skidded across the table to Paul.

Paul didn't want to touch the thing. Bridget could be really treacherous.

Cameron noticed that he didn't pick up the vial. It was empty but for any last drops that might remain. Abruptly, she laughed.

"What?" said Paul.

"You. You're so afraid. Everybody in the world laughs at love potions and thinks they don't work." Though Cameron also believed in the efficacy of the potions, she didn't find them to be a big deal.

"Everybody in the world didn't grow up with two *witches*," said Paul emphatically.

"It's not even a love potion," Cameron needled him, unable to resist. "Maybe you should see if there are a few drops in there for *your* emotional equilibrium."

"I'm not the one bursting into tears over a—" He stopped.

Cameron's eyebrows drew together. "A what?"

"He's so—preening. He belongs on cable. With his girl curls, that Jim Morrison do. It's hilarious."

Cameron pursed her lips briefly at this unfair description of Graham. She was beginning to enjoy herself. "You sound jealous."

"Of Graham Corbett?" To Paul's dismay, his voice cracked.

Cameron picked up the vial and carried it over to the stove. "What if I just put the last drop in your tea?"

"I won't drink it," he said, shaking his head.

Cameron rolled her eyes and set the vial near the sink to rinse and reuse for an herbal tincture. A pity that such an attractive man—and Paul was downright handsome—should be hopeless as a mate for anyone. Not because of anything to do with his faith in love potions. Just because he was so determinedly unattached. Which was childish.

A little catch in her heart warned her, cautioned her.

But she had nothing to fear from Paul. Not emotionally. Not in any way.

She vividly remembered four or so things about their Halloween encounter back in college. One—her own costume. Two—surprising tenderness, or maybe a tender surprise. Three—the glitter in his bed in the morning. Four—his announcing upon awakening that the sex would wreck their friendship. She knew that excuse was covered extensively in the useful book *He's Just Not That Into You*. Because it was a lie. It meant, *I don't want to have sex with you again*. Period.

Paul had rejected her. This permanently eliminated him from her pool of men with whom she might have an intimate relationship in the future.

As she was thinking this, he said, "You know what the Chinese remedy for lovesickness is?"

"What?" said Cameron without interest. There *was* no remedy.

"To make love with someone other than the object of your attraction."

Cameron eyed him suspiciously. "You're not propositioning me, are you?"

Paul hadn't been. He had been trying to goad her as she was goading him about the love potion. As far as he knew, Cameron hadn't been on a real date in years, and he'd been planning to suggest Sean Devlin as a possible choice. But now they'd entered murky waters. Possibly deep waters.

He didn't know Cameron's entire sexual history, but knew she'd done more than her share of fending off unwelcome advances on dates. He thought of her, in a brief unspoken second, more like a breath, of someone innocent and vulnerable, the girl he used to surf with, kick Hacky Sack with, toss a Frisbee with. One night she'd been in his bed, full-breasted, so sexual, so *different*. Now, suddenly, she was both those things. And he felt protective toward her.

He tried to answer and couldn't. Sleeping with Cameron… He liked the idea and also thought it was a mistake, not part of his plans. But he felt a curiosity, curiosity about who she was now, what they might be together. And his mouth said, "It's an idea."

Cameron almost gasped with the shock of it.

It was unthinkable.

She and Paul were friends, just friends. In any case, she liked sex, but she wasn't much into the sport of it, and what he was suggesting sounded like sport. Suppose she did it, would this Chinese cure work? She wasn't in any danger of falling in love with Paul.

A shudder swept over her with her next thought, a thought she tried to suppress.

Cameron was terrified of pregnancy. There were good reasons for this, several. And she knew her fear was irrational. But it was a fear that had *many* times made her decide not to go home with someone she might otherwise have accepted. Which was crazy. Birth control *did* work. And she and Paul would use condoms. It would be fine.

That's always what you think, Cameron, and then the next day you freak out.

But it was nonsense. She'd talked about it in therapy. She could handle that fear. Because it wasn't rational, and she was a very rational woman. Which left only the question of sex as sport. "I'm not the kind of woman who does things like that," she said emphatically. She took honey from the cupboard, leaving the door open.

Paul noticed that she had considered.

She said, "Want some toast?"

"Sure. Things like what?"

"Casual sex." She popped two slices of rye bread into the toaster.

"I wasn't thinking casual," Paul said. Though he'd accepted his share of invitations from eager women, the idea of "friends with benefits" slightly offended him. Sex was sex, friends were friends, lovers were rare. "More of a—" he sought for the right words, and found some he thought would appeal to her pro-therapy, talk-everything-through outlook "—healing experience."

"Like last time," she couldn't stop herself from saying, "when you *rejected* me in the morning? I haven't forgotten, you know."

"Rejected you?" He frowned, eyebrows drawing together.

"You said it would ruin our friendship or something like that."

Paul considered. "I do kind of remember that." What had been in his head? he wondered now. Probably his inherent dislike of denigrating friends to "friends with benefits." But why hadn't he wanted more with Cameron, a real relationship? At the time, she would have made an excellent girlfriend.

Now, since the subject had come up, it was beginning to occur to him that he wanted to know Cameron as a lover. Again. He had some memories of the night they'd spent together, but they were mostly visual. "I think it would make you feel better," he said, unable to keep from smiling. Feeling mischief sweep over him. "If it doesn't work the first time, we'll do it again. We'll do it until we cure—" he found he couldn't utter Graham Corbett's name "—your affliction."

"I'm not afflicted." Spinning back toward the toaster, she banged into the open cabinet door and cried out. She swore, it hurt so much.

She heard Paul get up from the table and bit down tears.

He turned her around and said, "Let's get you some ice. Looks like you're going to have a shiner."

"Great," she gasped through the pain.

Spontaneously, he kissed the tip of her nose. But then his lips drifted to her cheek, down to her mouth.

At first, she did not respond, and he was about to move away when she began kissing him back.

He could smell the bread toasting, but he'd lost all interest in food.

She kissed him. She felt his mouth open slightly, and so did hers. She felt the tip of his tongue caress her lips. She whispered, "Okay."

Paul let her body settle against his, touch everywhere, let her feel what was happening to him because of her.

His mind spun, seeing the teenage tomboy she'd been, the vulnerable person she still was inside, the lover he didn't really know.

I SHOULDN'T BE doing this, she thought minutes later in the bedroom. Abandoning the toast which had popped up, they had gone straight to her bed.

What if this wrecked her relationship with Paul?

Well, maybe that would be for the best. It would be better if Cameron had nothing more to do with any member of the Cureux family—not midwife and love-potion brewer Clare, not her antiseptically skeptical obstetrician ex-husband David, not witch-in-waiting Bridget and not Paul.

But Cameron liked Paul. And he was a friend, a friend who didn't mind if she woke him in the middle of night to drive Mariah to the vet because she'd eaten a tampon. She sometimes thought Paul would do anything for her. When she someday had a relationship with a man, she wanted it to be someone who would open up to her, talk to her about everything. But that wasn't Paul. Their friendship wasn't the talking kind but the being-together kind.

And sometimes she really wished she knew what went on in his head, what he *really* felt, the unspoken things.

And he wasn't talking now.

He took off her clothes, and she liked this. It felt strangely…forbidden. Tossing his own T-shirt to the floor beside Mariah, he gazed down at Cameron. "You are fantastically beautiful."

"What?" Her jaw actually dropped, and she found

herself trying to assume a persona, trying not to be aware that she was naked and he was looking at her, clearly intent on only one thing. Having her.

She quavered. The air felt so revealing. It swam between them. She reached up to his jeans, and he gently caught her wrists, placing them back against the sheets. "Slower," he said, and she felt the power of his intense maleness, his oppositeness from her.

He came down to her, to kiss her lips, to touch her face and her jaw.

Cameron believed herself to be jaded. During the years before Beatrice's pregnancy and birth, before she'd acquired her own terror of pregnancy and birth, she'd had some wildness. Encounters on the spur of the moment, a live-in boyfriend who'd been not very nice in the long run. Certain words from the mouths of men made her laugh, generally promises that they were going to send her to a yet unknown Eden of ecstasy. They had often made themselves ridiculous to her, and through her work she often found them unworthy of respect, earning only her contempt.

But Paul, in this minute, seemed a fairy-man, a god-man, a pagan creature who was pure desire and impervious to ridicule or derision. She realized, acutely, why they had never done this again. It was too much, too perfect, too close to what-should-be. Too utterly terrifyingly near her ultimate desire in a lover.

His body was beautiful, and she tried again to touch, this time, his shoulders.

He let her, briefly, then removed her hands from him again as he kissed her throat, her heart, her breasts…

Myrtle Hollow

CLARE CUREUX sat in her cabin, drinking the herbal infusion that would relax her, allowing her to sleep after the birth she'd just attended. Few people in Logan County chose homebirths these days. It used to be a choice of poverty, but now the indigent had help from the government to go to the hospital.

Ladonna Naggy's homebirth had been an educated choice. Ladonna had attended Yale, studied biology and was thinking of becoming a midwife herself. Bridget had come along to this birth as Clare's assistant, and Ladonna and her partner, Michel, had given birth to a beautiful son. Everything had gone right. Bridget had talked less than usual—this was something Clare had counseled her daughter about, because chatter could distract and irritate a woman in labor. Yes, Bridget was learning; after all, she had two children of her own.

Clare knew she herself was unlike other women, though she shared many of their experiences. Sixty-seven years old, divorced, mother of two, grandmother of two. She was a midwife and an herbalist, and some people called her a witch.

Clare was Irish on her mother's side, of Caribbean descent on her father's, her paternal grandmother having been white enough to "pass." Clare was not sure where "the Sight" came from, whether from Ireland or the Caribbean, but she had it, as did her daughter Bridget, her youngest. Clare had received the love potion recipe from her father's mother but brewed the recipe without the elaborate rituals her grandmother thought vital.

Grand-mère's view had been that if one did not make a sacrifice willingly, a sacrifice would be taken.

Clare refused to see that anything had been sacrificed in her life. Divorce from David? What had happened before the divorce? Just the price of her vocation—or so it had all seemed at the time.

The children believed that she and David had simply ceased getting along. Clare was content with this interpretation of the story, which had the advantage of being true, as far as it went.

But Paul, she knew, considered the explanation inadequate. And he used its so-called inadequacy to justify his own absurd belief that it was impossible for two people to remain married. Well, he claimed that he could never have such a partnership.

She sometimes wondered if knowing the whole truth would change Paul's mind. It was academic. He never *would* know, of course, because David would never tell him and neither would she. It hadn't been her finest hour; and if her son ever learned the truth, Paul would see it just as David had.

When given the choice, she'd chosen her vocation over her marriage. It had been selfish. But as she shut off the light in the kitchen and made her way through the dark cabin, reflecting on the birth she'd just been honored to witness, she was content.

CHAPTER TWO

CAMERON SOMETIMES thought she was actually insane. She considered her insanity as she crawled beneath her bed to retrieve the third used condom.

Paul had left all three wrappers on her bedside table, from where Mariah had stolen them and taken them to her bed.

Glad that Paul had been forced to go to the zoo, glad that nothing on Earth would come between him and his job, Cameron took her find into the bathroom to join the other two, turned on the water and prepared to make sure that every condom had kept its integrity. It was the kind of fanatical thing that an insane person might do, and Cameron had been told by various people that her fear of pregnancy was insane.

She didn't care. She had been in the middle of her monthly cycle last night—only peak fertility could have made her behave so stupidly—and she would be happier by day and night if she knew that not one of these three condoms had a hole in it.

Strange, she had not been terrified by pregnancy last night. And maybe she was distracting herself now from something a bit more frightening than bringing forth children in pain. Paul. She remembered *every* detail of the night before. She absolutely did not want to be cured from her infatuation with Graham Corbett by falling in love with someone so avowedly against commitment as Paul Cureux.

She was trying to talk herself out of actually making sure the condoms had no holes when she heard someone call her name. "Cameron! Cameron!"

Not Mary Anne. Cameron was glad of that. If her cousin had slept with Graham Corbett—and why wouldn't she have done so—she wouldn't come around and tell Cameron about it. No, this was the voice of Cameron's younger sister, Denise. Denise, unlike Beatrice and Cameron, had inherited a normal physiognomy that would allow normal childbearing. She was a student at West Virginia University but home for the weekend.

Her little sister, with no respect for privacy, appeared in the bathroom door. "What are you doing?" said Denise. "My God, who hit you?"

"I walked into a cabinet door." Cameron tossed the condoms in the trash.

Denise's face filled with alarm. "No, you didn't. You tell me people always say that when someone hit them."

Cameron *had* told her that, basing the statement on her experience working with battered women. "I turned around in the kitchen and whacked the cabinet door. I'd never let anyone hit me."

Unfortunately, Denise's acceptance of the truth allowed her to return to her original question. "Were you washing out condoms?"

"Of course not. What do you want?"

"You asked me to join you for your Women of Strength herb walk, if you remember."

Every weekend, Cameron planned something for Women of Strength, a program she'd instituted at the Women's Resource Center to help battered women regain their self-confidence through physical activity. Sometimes it was a caving expedition, sometimes a self-defense class, sometimes a bicycle ride or hike.

"I'm sick. I might have to beg off," Cameron said. She was sick because it *was* absurd to think she might have become pregnant despite birth control, but it was far from absurd that after such a very interesting—such a truly *great* night—with Paul, she could hardly think of anything but him. Never, *never,* had she experienced anything like it.

"You're never sick," said Denise.

The herb walk might distract her from Paul—if only any woman but his mother were leading it. Well, there was no begging off. She murmured, "True," with distraction and hoped fervently that Clare could not or at least *would* not read her mind.

"IF A PERSON has already drunk a love potion, what happens if someone gives them a different one?" Cameron asked Clare Cureux. Because Graham Corbett had drunk a love potion, and he was now in love with Mary Anne. That he'd never been the intended recipient of the potion was moot. And Graham Corbett would *still* be a much better choice for Cameron than…

Don't think about him.

Paul's mother, her gray-threaded hair in one long braid, glared at Cameron. "Who are you talking about? Not that radio—"

"No one," Cameron insisted. "It's just theoretical." In fact, she still couldn't help fearing that Clare, who had "the Sight," might somehow know what had transpired the night before with her only son. These questions were Cameron's way of trying to distract Clare, to make Clare think that Cameron was focused on Graham.

Which she wasn't at the moment. She *did* feel differently about Graham after sleeping with Paul.

"The answer is that nothing would happen. Nothing." Clare gave her another irritated look. Though Clare sold love potions, she did so reluctantly, always trying to talk the buyer out of it first. *Let nature take its course,* was her unchanging advice.

Bridget said, "How is it going, by the way, Cameron?"

No doubt she thought her question suitably vague. Cameron made a noncommittal gesture with her hand. So-so.

Now, mother cast an appalled look at daughter, then coldly turned away.

"It wasn't a love potion," Cameron interjected.

She hadn't been thrilled to find that Paul's sister was along on this walk. Cameron felt edgy enough in Clare's presence without the danger of Bridget's sometimes greater perceptiveness.

Cameron was surprised so many women were interested in herbs. Four had turned out for the first herb walk and eight for this one, not including Cameron, Denise, Clare or Bridget.

Bridget tossed her long dreadlocks and said, almost reverently, "*Coltsfoot*. Look, Mom."

Cameron stepped back to let the other women, three of whom had left abusive spouses and taken refuge at the Women's Resource Center's "safe house," come in closer to see the plant and hear Clare describe its medicinal properties. Like nearly everyone else on the walk, these women had wanted to know who hit Cameron, if she was in trouble, what they could do, how she could let this happen to her. They seemed skeptical that she'd actually walked into a cabinet door.

Cameron thought she might lose her job over this black eye. She was supposed to be helping women to escape from abusive situations, and now her clients thought she was lying about how she'd gotten hurt.

Clare didn't suspect her of lying. When Cameron had explained, she'd simply sniffed and told her the sort of poultice she should have applied at once.

Another memory of the night before—more a question—*What had Paul really felt?*—needled her. She had to stop thinking about the night before. It was nothing to get romantic about. She tried to distract herself with the fear of pregnancy, the illusion of a tiny hole. Surely a meaningful amount of sperm couldn't get through. There was no way.

Of course, it was Paul's father, David, a former obstetrician, who had once redefined competition to Cameron, when she was stressing over her chances before a 10K.

"My dear, as I am constantly reminding my children, you are the sperm that made it. You'll never face competition like that again."

She didn't care. It was a silly fear. And if she got pregnant, it was only what women had been doing forever, what women's bodies were made for.

Had she been crazy to sleep with Paul? She could not afford to feel this way about him. She needed to be *normal* with him. If he thought she felt romantically toward him— She almost winced at the thought of it. Being in love with Paul would be a hundred times worse than being in love with Graham.

Chief Logan State Park Zoo

PAUL HAD FOUGHT as hard as anyone to get the pair of pale-faced saki monkeys to the zoo. What was more, he'd managed his fight the old-fashioned way, schmoozing with wealthy individuals who might become zoo benefactors. He'd wanted no part of his boss's "Hold A Baby Snow Leopard" money-making scheme.

He was, at this time, head keeper of primates. In the past, Paul had worked in reptiles and with the felids, but for the past four years he'd worked with the zoo's ringtailed lemurs, black howler monkeys and chimpanzees. He found it difficult to go home at night sometimes because he was attached to these animals.

A grad student named Helena Ruffles was doing research with one of their chimps, a three-year-old female named Portia. Paul loved to watch Portia learn words.

Portia loved Paul, who had known her since she was a
baby. In fact, he often said that Portia was his favorite
female.

But not at the moment.

What he wanted most of all was to make love with
Cameron again. She was an astoundingly good-looking
woman. He'd always thought so. Her face didn't have
Mary Anne's model's bones, but her smile melted his
heart. Seeing her gave him the same feeling as diving into
the river in the summer, going barefoot in damp grass,
picking up his custom guitar.... However, what he'd always felt for her was friendship, and now he wondered
why. It bothered him that Cameron had drunk something
Bridget had given her, but *he* hadn't accepted a drink
from Bridget lately, not even a glass of water.

His father, long divorced from Paul's mother, was an
utter skeptic when it came to the love potions. Paul
wished he could be a skeptic.

Paul did not want to be married. Women were treacherous and powerful, and he preferred a bachelor's existence. So he wasn't sure he should make love with
Cameron again. Cameron was...sensitive. The local per-
ception of her was of a man-hating champion of women's
rights, directing the Women's Resource Center. Paul
himself sometimes accused her of being that way. But on
some subjects, she had the heart of a marshmallow. And
her favorite reading material was pre-1960 romance
fiction.

Paul found saki hair below the trees. Was the male still
pulling hairs out of his tail? He glanced up, hunting for

the primates, and found the male doing just that. Paul slipped back into the keeper area and returned with several dog toys. He particularly liked the flying monkey toy that screamed when you shot it up into the trees. He sent it flying upward so that the male could go retrieve it.

The female got it instead.

The male pulled more hairs out of his tail. Paul threw a dog's Kong toy on the ground and also tossed out a plush gingerbread man, who promptly began singing, "Run, run, as fast as you can…"

He should at least go by Cameron's after work. Just to…reestablish normality.

CAMERON HAD RIDDEN her bike to the trailhead for the herb walk, and she rode her bike home afterward. During a brief stop at the grocery store, a patron of the Women's Resource Center asked, suspiciously, what had happened to her face.

She went home and found Paul's quarter-ton pickup truck in front of her house beside her own ancient Datsun. As she began adjusting to the fact that Paul was inside, Wolfie and Mariah met her on the porch. Cameron petted Mariah, and Wolfie and Cameron looked at each other, the dog as wary as always.

She went inside, and Paul said from the kitchen, "I fed the dogs."

He was at the kitchen table, reading her newspaper and eating pesto straight from the jar.

"Are you going to save me some of that?" she snapped.

"Your eye looks horrible."

Cameron found she was shaking. She was shaking because she'd made love with Paul the night before and now he was in her house and she didn't know how to behave around him. She found it terrifying that her most recurring thoughts of the day had been of him—nothing else. The minutiae of Paul and of the night before. Every single word and touch exchanged. It was absurd.

So now she didn't say "What are you doing here?" because she was slightly glad that he *was* there, although she didn't want to be glad. She'd barely thought of Graham all day. She'd thought of Paul.

"Thank you for feeding the dogs." Wolfie ate outside and only when he thought no one was looking. Mariah had followed her into the house and sat politely beside Paul, looking hopeful. She had a beautiful black-and-brown face and fluffy black fur that had remained puppy-soft even as she matured.

Cameron managed to ask, "Why did you come over?"

He looked up, dark eyes wide, and it occurred to her that what other women—her cousin, Mary Anne, for instance— had been telling her for years was true. Paul was a hunk. He had one of those hard-jawed faces that you sometimes saw on guys who climbed Everest. The hint of five o'clock shadow, though undoubtedly uncomfortable for anyone who kissed him, increased the sexy mountain-man effect.

She wished she could stop trembling.

"To see how your day went," he replied calmly.

"Everyone asked who hit me," she informed him.

He winced slightly, almost as though *he* had hit her.

It was an unusually sympathetic response from Paul.

Normally he would have said that it would help bond her with her clients, or something equally thoughtless. But he seemed to appreciate how bad it was for the director of the Women's Resource Center to walk around with a black eye.

"Denise is coming over," she said. "For dinner. You can stay." She went out to her bicycle to collect the groceries she'd bought and bring them inside.

As Cameron began slicing vegetables, she noticed that Paul had made no attempt to touch or kiss her. She kept thinking of the way he'd kissed her the night before, not opening his mouth at first, just gradually doing so, just tasting her lips with his tongue, as though it was something he'd never done before.

So, we're going back to being just friends, she thought. Maybe he thought they'd be "friends with privileges" or bonking buddies. Not a chance.

From the table, Paul watched her back, the two light brown braids swinging over the shoulders of her thrift-shop Fair Isle sweater. He could say something about last night. But what was there to say?

He wanted to do it again.

What he said was, "I don't want to hurt you."

At the counter, Cameron froze. Of all the things a man could say after a sexual encounter, this was one of the worst. Implicit was the fact that his hurting her was quite possible. In fact, it implied a certain likelihood. Attempting objectivity, she compared "I don't want to hurt you" to "Sex will ruin our friendship." Hard to judge which was worse, actually. What was she supposed to say?

She wheeled around. "You can't hurt me, because I'm not sleeping with you again. For one thing, I don't want to get pregnant." She wished she hadn't said that, for many reasons, from hating to discuss a terrifying subject to hating to tell lies. "But even if being pregnant wouldn't kill me, you and I are just friends. What happened happened, but now my biggest concern is learning how to conceal a black eye before I lose my job." *Since I've already lost my mind and slept with you.*

Paul thought she was acting strangely, but she'd been clear. He told himself it was a relief. And though the thought of her becoming pregnant alarmed him almost as much as it could alarm her, he knew that any fear of that outcome was neurotic. He said, "This is the twenty-first century. It's totally irrational to believe you will die in childbirth."

Her face flushed in a way he associated with her being particularly—well, hysterical. *Oh, God, here we go.*

"Easy for you to say! Didn't one of your own mother's clients almost die in childbirth?"

"No. It was a stillbirth, what you're talking about, and it happened at the hospital." Actually, Paul wasn't sure of this. It had happened when he was six years old, and his father had moved out soon afterward. Sometimes the story of the stillbirth came up when people argued that homebirths were unsafe. He thought he could remember his mother saying, "If she'd been my client, I would have sent her to a physician." But Paul didn't know why this was, knew none of the details, though he was sure either of his parents could provide them.

Cameron was still talking. "Anyhow, you think dying in childbirth is the only unpleasant possibility. You think, 'Oh, they'll just give her an epidural. She'll be fine.' Roxanne Jacobs had an epidural, and she's had crippling back pain ever since. You think, 'Oh, Cameron will just have a cesarean section.' My sister *miscarried* in the fifth month *four times*. You think a little miscarriage is nothing, but that's like a stillbirth every time."

Paul considered interrupting, but it was hard to find a place.

"And each time was physically excruciating. She thought she was going to die, not to mention being heart-broken because she'd lost the baby. And they *are* babies, premature but completely babies. Beatrice named every one." Tears welled in Cameron's eyes.

Horrified, Paul said, "Baby—" He almost put his hand over his mouth. He'd called her "baby." That could lead to lack of clarity. About their relationship. But he forced himself to finish saying what he'd begun to say. "You know how you get before your period. You're just freak—"

"I AM NOT EXPECTING MY PERIOD!" she shrieked. "Would I be worried if I was? Do you know *nothing* about women?"

He considered asking her to please put down the knife but decided to remain silent.

He heard the front door open. Denise called, "Cameron?"

Thank God, he thought.

Cameron grabbed a dishcloth to wipe her eyes.

Two days later

CAMERON PEERED around the Charleston Walmart as she waited in line, clutching a magazine on top of her two-in-one, double-check home pregnancy kit. Paul was not with her, having dropped her at Walmart and gone alone to prowl the endless aisles at Home Depot. That night, he was going to be the soundman for an English band called Crawl at a Charleston concert, and he'd asked her to go with him, and she'd agreed. So, though this was the Charleston Walmart, it was not out of the realm of possibility that she would see someone from Logan here.

With the coast clear, she went through the checkout, smiling tensely at the clerk. She paid for her purchases, then hurried into the ladies' restroom, where she closed herself in a cubicle to find out the worst.

Alone, she watched the test strip, prepared to wait the three minutes, waiting to exhale in relief.

One line appeared, confirming that the test was working.

Nothing else.

She waited.

She looked at her watch.

She tried to breathe. *It's okay. It's okay.*

She wasn't pregnant.

She waited for relief to wash over her, but relief wasn't precisely what she felt. She *was* relieved, of course she was. But—well, it must be the biological clock thing. She'd been terrified by the possibility that she was pregnant, or she'd never have bought a test. But she'd had a sort of excitement, a sort of pleasure, in thinking she and Paul might have conceived a child.

Which was silly. She threw away the first test, stuck the second in her purse to take home, and washed her hands. There was really no way that pregnancy could have been good news. Even if she'd been pregnant, she'd have been likely to miscarry. This would save her so much heartache.

There was no reason for her to be depressed.

But she considered telling Paul she wasn't feeling well, that she had run into friends and would make her own way home from Charleston. He could go to this gig on his own, a gig that epitomized everything about him that refused to grow up. He worked in the zoo to support his career as a musician and worked as a soundman to help pay for his equipment. Of course, he *should* be a musician. And he did love his job at the zoo. Okay, she was being hard on him, but she needed to keep her distance from Paul for the time being.

The thing is that she'd sort of, almost kind of, wished she was pregnant. It would have been a *catastrophe*. There was no way it could have turned out well. Paul would never have married her, and she didn't think she would have wanted him to. Permanent children did not marry, and the thought of Peter Pan being a father to anyone but the Lost Boys was both ludicrous and scary.

No, she'd go to the Crawl show and be friendly. Paul was no threat to the peace of her heart.

But as she emerged from the ladies' room, she collided with someone entering the men's. She looked up into the handsome and obviously delighted face of Sean Devlin.

"HOW DID YOU MEET these guys anyway?" Sean asked Paul, looking around the nearly empty club where roadies and members of Crawl were setting up. Sean had paid the cover charge, telling Cameron he was interested in young bands.

Paul pretended he hadn't heard. He was angry at Cameron, who had explained Sean's following them to the club with, *It's okay. I told him you and I aren't really together.*

He'd told her it was *not* okay to tell random people from Logan that they weren't really together.

She wore jeans and a brown long-sleeved T-shirt, with her hair in braids. Paul didn't know that she'd deliberately dressed down to emphasize to herself that she and Paul weren't really dating, that they were friends and her presence here tonight was all part of the sham they'd developed.

A roadie walked past in a T-shirt showing their first CD, *In the Name of Fear.*

"Facebook," Paul finally answered Sean. "I met Angus." The bass player. "He sent me a CD, and now I'm a fan. Also, he came to see me play in Logan at the campaign party, before the election. We talked then, and I said I'd do sound for them at this gig and the one in Morgantown Wednesday."

Cameron, aware that Paul wasn't keen on Sean's presence, asked him, "Want anything to drink?"

"Some orange juice. Something nonalcoholic. It should be on the house."

"I'll get it," Sean offered. He looked down at Cameron from his towering six foot three. "And what can I get you?"

"The same, please."

When Sean had gone, Paul said, "Why did you ask him?"

"I thought the band would appreciate more people coming."

"Plenty of people *are* coming." Sean had been allowed in early only because he was with Paul and Cameron.

"Well, you won't be able to talk to me or dance with me," Cameron pointed out. "Sean can."

"No doubt." He managed to mutter, "Thanks," as Sean handed him a glass of orange juice, after giving Cameron's to her.

The club began to fill, and when Crawl finally came on, Cameron was pleasantly surprised by the music, which showed both originality and the influence of many other groups she liked. She danced with Sean, not far from where Paul worked the soundboard, because it was farther from the speakers in front. Sean seemed to share her opinion on avoiding the speakers, and he also seemed disinterested in dancing with anyone else.

At the break, he escorted her outside, where they watched other people smoke. "I used to," Sean admitted, watching the smokers enviously. He shook his head.

"It's hard to quit, isn't it?" Cameron asked.

"Miserable. But I was going through counseling, and that helped—a bit. Some of the things that come up just make you want to smoke more."

Therapy! Cameron wanted to shout. This man had

had therapy! No wonder she could talk so easily to Sean. He wasn't all masculine barriers, all inaccessible emotions, all defensive silence.

He asked her about her job, and he told her about his and about his avocations, writing plays and poetry.

Cameron said she'd like to read some of his poetry sometime.

He said he'd like that. "I was reluctant to—you know— pursue it," he said. "I thought you were in a relationship."

Cameron thrust away the memory of sleeping with Paul that one night. "Well, I'm not. And you?"

He shook his head. "Divorced. After that was when I decided on some counseling."

"That's a very mature choice," she told him and confessed that she'd gone the same road after a tough experience with a man with whom she'd lived.

Sean said, "So—is Paul going to drive you home?"

Cameron thought guiltily that it was because of Paul that she'd gotten into the gig free. "Yes," she said definitely. "I actually am his date."

He nodded. "I'll be gone this week on some teacher training, but I'll call you as soon as I'm back."

PAUL FOUND her presence distracting. He had always liked the way Cameron danced, but it had never affected him so strongly, and he didn't care to see how strongly Sean Devlin was affected, too. Paul remembered making love with her. What bothered him in retrospect, as—he admitted now—it had bothered him then, was that she preferred Graham Corbett.

Never doing that again, he thought. She was preoccupied still, probably still mooning over the radio personality. Yet as he watched her dancing to the music of Crawl, her expression distant but also, to him, vulnerable, his heart tore in all directions. How did he feel about her, say, hooking up with Sean Devlin? Becoming Sean's girlfriend?

Frankly, Paul hated the idea. Sean was an all right guy and good-looking, anyone would admit that. But Cameron was *his,* Paul's, best friend. Her falling in love and marrying someone like Sean—not a good idea at all.

He shouldn't have invited her along. There was no reason. He'd just wanted to show her that no matter what, he still cared for her, still wanted to be around her. He'd wanted to prove that they remained friends.

Or something like that.

Did he want Cameron for his own girlfriend?

No. Of course not. Definitely not. He didn't want a girlfriend. First you had a girlfriend, then you had someone who wanted to marry you. Perhaps someone who would want you to find a different job, a job that paid more. And someone who would insist on a certain way of being that would ultimately destroy the magic of life.

At least Cameron wasn't in love with him.

That was good, he told himself. Best for her, best for him. Best all around.

After the final set, after the fans had screamed and stomped the floor and begged the band for one more, Cameron chatted with them while they moved equipment and Sean dogged her like a shadow. Paul saw the band liked her, even seemed to like Sean, and he felt left out, forgotten by Cameron. Later, he found her waiting in his car, reading a novel with his headlamp, which she had borrowed.

"Where did Sean go?"

"Home." She didn't look up.

"And how is *Jane Eyre* on the two thousandth reading?" he asked.

Her eyes remained fixed on the page. "If you had a modicum of education, you would know that *Jane Eyre* is the story of a self-centered older man, who dislikes children, deceiving a vulnerable woman twenty years his junior. After she learns that he is actually married and keeps his first wife, whom *he* claims is insane, locked in an attic, he continues to attempt seducing her and she continues to love him, and after he is blind and crippled and his wife dead under mysterious circumstances, the female protagonist returns to him. It's a creepy story, and one reading, in school, was enough for me."

Paul reached across the front seat, lifted the cover of her book slightly. A novel by someone named Emilie Loring. It was entitled *My Dearest Love,* and the woman on the front looked like Elizabeth Taylor. Familiar with Cameron's reading material, he suspected it had been published sometime between 1920 and 1960.

Cameron ignored him.

He started the car, plugged his iPod into the dash, and put on some music. Cameron recognized the start of "So Alone," by Rhesus. Paul had given her the English band's CD *Narcolepsy Baby* two months earlier.

She told Paul, "Those guys—and girl—were sweet.

The band members. I think there's another band with the same name."

Paul nodded absently. "I think there may be."

More than an hour later, when he reached her house, she thanked him, and just for a second she glanced at him, and Paul wondered if she wanted him to kiss her. He *did* want to but knew better. If he did, she would become his girlfriend, and that would herald a world of things he did not want.

But then he thought he'd imagined the look. She got out, and he let her. Made himself let her go.

Myrtle Hollow

CLARE CUREUX woke with a start.

The dream had been horrible. It was Flower Patten all over again, but this time, that case of true cephalopelvic disproportion, CPD, had been Cameron McAllister's, and it was Cameron DOA at the hospital.

What a nightmare. Clare closed her eyes again, then reopened them.

Silly Cameron thought she was in love with Graham. Clare knew her dream had been no vision. She knew when something was an omen of the future, and this had been a nightmare, nothing more ominous.

The question was, why had she dreamed about Cameron and dreamed that Cameron was pregnant?

Thinking of Cameron made Clare think of Paul, and she frowned at the thought. Paul's life was his own, but

he certainly lived for himself to a greater degree than
she'd have liked.

Which had to be something she'd caused, that selfishness, that fierce…well…*childishness*.

She breathed relief. Just a nightmare. Cameron was *not*
pregnant.

CHAPTER THREE

FIVE DAYS LATER, Cameron, glancing in the mirror as she dressed for work, thought her nipples looked larger than usual. There could be no reason for this. Theoretically, it could occur because of pregnancy. But pregnancy didn't show signs this early, and she wasn't pregnant.

Still, she decided to use the second pregnancy test.

She knew it would say that she wasn't pregnant, and then she could forget about the optical illusion she'd just had and also completely forget about making love with Paul, which she was having trouble forgetting.

She wished Paul was the kind of man she could be in a relationship with.

She thought of Mary Anne, in love now with Graham Corbett. Cameron knew Mary Anne *was* in love, and in *their* case the attraction had begun on Graham's side. A fairy-tale romance. *Why can't it happen to me?*

Briefly, Cameron considered Sean Devlin. How bizarre that she felt so little attraction to him. And he was just what she should want. They had talked so easily at the Crawl gig. He'd been willing to tell her of his vulnerability following his divorce, even tendencies he might have picked up from the kind of childhood he'd had. But there seemed, to her, no spark between them— not on her side, anyway. Maybe she wasn't ready to have a lasting relationship. Her job had made her appreciate the freedom of not having to adapt to another person's wants, schedule, whims. But *selfishness* wasn't the reason she felt no attraction to Sean. And they'd been great friends in college, too.

Paul, however...

Sometimes, sometimes when she saw Paul's name and number come up on her cell phone, she felt an overwhelming comfort that she thought must be what people felt in good marriages. No—more than comfort. Different than comfort. Attraction. Attraction to Paul—that frightened her. Paul, like Rhett Butler, was "not a marrying man."

In the bathroom, she used the pregnancy kit and set it on the sink ledge, went into the kitchen and found a banana for breakfast and returned to the bathroom and the sight of two thin lines.

She remembered, in panic, the mild disappointment she'd felt in the restroom at the Charleston Walmart. What had prompted such insanity?

But despite her fears—of being pregnant, of losing the pregnancy because of an inability to carry a child, of loving the child and perhaps losing it—she couldn't deny some private pleasure. She was, at this moment, a mother. She didn't understand her own feelings but she well guessed the reason for them.

It was because *this* child was also Paul Cureux's.

SEAN CALLED later that day and asked if she wanted to meet for coffee.

Cameron was abruptly off coffee but promised to meet him at the coffeehouse anyhow. She would order herbal tea.

When she entered the Chief Logan Coffeehouse and saw Sean stand up, she almost gasped at how absolutely handsome he was. Breathtaking. Truly one of the best-looking men she'd ever seen.

Maybe she *was* attracted.

He got their drinks—double cappuccino for himself, raspberry leaf tea for her—and joined her at a table by the window, out of hearing range of the other patrons.

He was easy to talk to, told her about his marriage and the ex-wife who was a model. He'd brought her a chap-book of his poems, for which she thanked him.

Watching her with great penetration, he said at last, "I think there's something on your mind."

Cameron knew that he was someone who could keep a secret, knew because he had been that way in the past. So she said the requisite words. "I'll tell you, but you can't say anything to *anyone.*"

"Of course."

And she told him. His mouth fell open slightly, and he gazed at her with an expression of wonder. His dark brown hair was going prematurely gray, but his eyebrows remained extremely dark and bushy. "When are you going to tell him?"

Cameron shook her head. "Not yet." She wouldn't mention the possibility of miscarriage because she could no longer *acknowledge* that possibility, even to herself.

It was unthinkable. And if she didn't think of it, it could not happen.

Sean gave her a very serious look. "You should tell him, Cam."

"I will. Just…not yet."

SEAN CALLED every day and became Cameron's confidant. Cameron really wasn't surprised that he hadn't been put off by the reality of her carrying another man's child. She'd seen men who were just terribly attracted to mothers, and maybe Sean was one of these. Some of these, Cameron felt, were looking for a second mother for themselves, but she couldn't believe Sean fit into this category. In any case, Sean was not an object. Paul was the man who interested her—and she didn't *want* him to interest her.

Paul and she always talked daily, but now Cameron found herself avoiding him. Besides, whenever he brought up Sean—which he always did—they ended up sniping at each other. But it was nearly Thanksgiving before she had a heart-to-heart with her cousin, on the telephone, and felt no jealousy when she learned that Mary Anne *had* indeed slept with Graham Corbett—only relief at finally speaking with her best friend. Cameron was again astonished by her own reaction. She no longer cared. Not remotely. Cameron could picture Graham in her mind's eye—the tall body, the curly dark hair—she could imagine his voice, that radio voice—she could imagine all these things beside her tall, model-beautiful cousin with no discernible feeling. Was she actually *over* him? She didn't realize she'd spoken out loud until Mary Anne replied.

"You mean, Bridget's potion *worked?*"

Cameron now wondered if the draught Bridget had given her *had* been a love potion, so she wasn't impressed with Paul's sister at the moment. After briefly excoriating Bridget, she invited Mary Anne to go caving with her Thanksgiving weekend—a Women of Strength outing. Big Jim Cave was at the state park. Maybe Cameron would go by the zoo afterward. Maybe she'd do what Sean kept urging her to do and tell Paul…. It took Mary Anne's mentioning her own "suffering" because days had passed without Graham calling to bring Cameron out of her reverie.

Suffering made Cameron think of her sister Beatrice giving birth and of her own pregnancy. It all came out then. Cameron admitted that she was pregnant, avoided mentioning the father and used Mary Anne's sudden burst of compassion—for Mary Anne knew how terrified Cameron was of pregnancy and birth—to persuade Mary Anne to go caving.

Cameron, who had been talking on one of the lines at the Women's Resource Center, abruptly feared that somebody might have overheard, that she shouldn't have said out loud that she was pregnant. Because she had not yet told Paul. Wasn't sure how—or even *if*—to tell him. What if he thought her silly for doing a pregnancy test, because it was so early? What if *he* believed she wanted to be pregnant with his child?

In any case, she was alone at the Women's Resource Center, catching up on work—checking statistics for a grant writer who was trying to get more funding for the center—and holding down the hotline until the scheduled volunteer showed up later that afternoon.

The hotline rang, and Cameron picked it up from her desk. "Women's Resource Center Helpline."

"Hi. Mm. I'm upset by something. Something my husband did."

"Yes?"

As she listened to the horror story that slowly unfolded, Cameron's skin began crawling. She felt a terrible anger toward the man who had treated his wife so shamefully.

"He says it's his right because he's my husband."

"He's wrong." Cameron questioned the woman about what she planned to do. *Nothing. I can't leave him, can I?*

Fifteen minutes later, when she was off the phone, Cameron wondered if her answering the helpline might be bad for her baby. Weren't you supposed to avoid negative emotions? And on the helpline, she listened to women in impossible situations, who truly believed there was no way out. The doubt and despair of rape, of violence, the constant echoing of *Was it my fault?*

She liked helping people, liked helping other women, and she knew she was good at it. She'd experienced enough unpleasantness in her life, seen enough, that she had compassion, that she knew bad things, or at least sad things, happened—eventually, to everyone. She'd been in bad situations with men, and what had been ghastly at the time had ultimately made her stronger.

But she wanted to do everything right for this baby, and she was only going to think positively about outcomes. Not for a second would she allow a negative thought to enter her head.

She wondered if it was too early to see a physician. Or a midwife.

Cameron believed that most women in the United States in particular—and especially their babies—were better off when birth happened at home. Hospitals routinely did things that made it difficult for women to labor and that compromised the health of the baby. The perfect example was the electronic fetal monitor. Hospitals used these, which forced a laboring woman to be on her back; the only worse position for giving birth would be standing on one's head. The weight of the baby then pressed down on the mother's vena cava, robbing the baby of blood and oxygen. Then fetal distress occurred.

But Cameron didn't have a normal pelvis. Well, she suspected she didn't, though she couldn't really judge for herself. She was built like Beatrice. After miscarriage number four, Beatrice had decided to have her baby at the hospital. The baby had been premature, so the best place *was* the hospital. Preemies should always be born in the hospital. They were so vulnerable with their organs not fully formed.

Cameron knew midwives, of course. Clare Cureux was a "lay" or direct-entry midwife, meaning she hadn't been to school to become a midwife, though she certainly was well-educated, her office filled with medical texts. And she went to workshops and conferences—or had done, for years. Bridget was thinking of going to school to become a certified nurse-midwife.

But Cameron couldn't go to the Cureux women because she hadn't yet told Paul she was pregnant.

She reached for the phone book to see who else she could find.

Thanksgiving
Myrtle Hollow

DAVID CUREUX had carved the turkey and was filling plates for the assembled family. Though he had divorced Clare more than two decades earlier, this was still his family: his eldest, Paul; his daughter, Bridget; Bridget's husband, Beau; their two children, Nick and Merrill; and Clare.

He and Paul had put the extra leaf in the table so that the entire family would fit.

Bridget said, "Couldn't Cameron make it?"

"She's with her family at her grandmother's house," Paul said, not liking something sly in Bridget's tone. He refused to encourage Bridget by asking what kind of concoction she'd brewed for Cameron or if it really had been innocuous, just something to help Cameron get over Graham Corbett.

Bridget was annoyed with him anyhow; she said he'd been insensitive in how he'd told her that she needed to watch Nick at the zoo when Nick was near the pond. Basic child safety! He hadn't thought tact was an issue. *Bridget, your kid could drown, hello?* Which wasn't what he'd said, admittedly.

His sister could hold a grudge for a lifetime.

Clare said, "We're supposed to get snow next week."

She spoke matter-of-factly. She loved to listen to weather reports. Though Clare had "the Sight" and knew some things in advance, she never knew what the weather would do except by listening to forecasters.

Bridget said, "Is her black eye gone?"

"Yes," Paul answered succinctly.

"How'd she get a black eye?" asked David.

"Walked into a cabinet door." Paul had given this explanation so many times that he'd begun to feel as though it *was* a lie. He did not want to talk about Cameron. Cameron was acting very strangely. She'd been avoiding him for two weeks. It reinforced that their sleeping together had been a mistake.

Bridget said, "Who's that hunk she's been hanging around with?"

Paul deliberately kept his face expressionless. "Someone we knew at school. Sean Devlin. New drama teacher at the high school."

He could feel his sister watching him as though expecting him to turn neon-green.

"Are they seeing each other?"

"How should I know?"

Bridget made a sound that could have expressed amusement or scorn or triumph. "Because you talk to her every day?"

"She doesn't talk to me about him."

Bridget seemed to have exhausted the topic, for she exclaimed suddenly to her mother, "Oh, did you hear about Lou Anne Shaw?"

"That was a travesty," her mother replied tartly.

Paul listened as Bridget described everything that had been done wrong by the local hospital for Lou Anne Shaw and her baby.

Paul's father remained uncharacteristically silent on the subject. He was not going to leap in and support the colleague in question, which meant, Paul decided, that he felt that the people at the hospital *had* made some mistakes.

"They should have sectioned her *right away*," exclaimed Bridget, an unusual point of view from a woman who'd grown up in a home where homebirth was considered the best way to have babies.

"Is everyone all right?" Paul finally asked, unable to forget Cameron's hysteria a couple of weeks earlier. Childbirth was normal. He knew that. And, of course, Cameron wasn't pregnant, would probably never *get* pregnant. But it seemed to him that labor and birth could be a risky business.

"Yes, everyone's fine," said Bridget. "No thanks to that quack."

Her father roused himself to make tut-tutting sounds.

As far as Paul could make out, the woman had been a true case of something called CPD, which seemed to be what Cameron thought she had. A pelvis too small for having babies. The woman, who'd grown up in Logan but had moved away and was receiving prenatal care elsewhere, came in with premature labor. The physician, rather than listening to anything she told him, said he'd have a nurse monitor her for a bit and see what happened. Or something of that nature.

It sounded like malpractice to Paul, and he reflected how he'd hated this aspect of his mother being a midwife, how sometimes his parents had traded horror stories across the table, some catastrophes seemingly caused by midwives, others by physicians. But he was curious about something. Not quite looking at his mother, he said, "Isn't that what happened with that lady back when we were little? Only the baby didn't make it?"

The table became unnaturally still and quiet.

Paul ignored this. "Why did that happen again?"

Clare said, "We'll talk about it later," in a very firm, quick voice that meant she wasn't going to discuss it over Thanksgiving dinner. Paul wondered if he'd been insensitive. The long-ago incident involved someone his mother had known, hadn't it? She had been involved.

But Clare said, "She wasn't my client," said it almost as though to herself.

CHAPTER FOUR

The caving trip

"YOU SHOULDN'T GO caving when you're pregnant," Mary Anne told Cameron as they waited in the parking lot of the Women's Resource Center to see if anyone showed up for the Women of Strength trip.

"Of course I can," Cameron replied.

It had taken Mary Anne approximately three seconds to guess that Paul must be the father of Cameron's baby. Asked bluntly, Cameron had been unable to lie. She'd been unmoved by Mary Anne's assertion that her little cousin was going to be beautiful. Mary Anne had hips made for childbearing, so of course she could be lighthearted.

"I'm going to see a midwife next week. She's in McDowell County," Cameron said tersely.

"Shouldn't you have an obstetrician? And if you're going to a midwife," Mary Anne asked, "why not Clare Cureux?"

Even Mary Anne knew that Cameron would be unable to give birth normally. Her inner panic intensifying in a familiar wave, Cameron said, "Yes, I probably will end up with an obstetrician, but I haven't seen anyone yet at all. So I'm starting with a midwife. But the point is to see a birth attendant in another county, for the time being. And I'm not going to the Cureux family for anything!"

"But you've got to tell—"

"I'm only a few days pregnant!"

Finally, one person showed for the trip, dashing Mary Anne's hopes that it could be called off. Angie Workman joined them in Mary Anne's car, and they headed for the State Park Zoo.

Cameron loved caving. She was small—thus made for caving—and had participated in several cave rescues over the years. Outside Big Jim Cave, while they suited up in coveralls, helmets and headlamps, Cameron gave her standard rules-of-caving lecture on protecting the cave environment, light sources, general safety.

Then they started into the cave. It wasn't one of Cameron's favorite grottoes, but it was free of tight passages. Mary Anne hated those. Angie, who was built on Cameron's scale, exclaimed over the beauty of the cave.

It happened when they reached Boulder Gulch.

Mary Anne stepped on a boulder, and it rolled. Once.

Cameron heard the sound and spun around as her cousin tumbled over the edge of the area into a crevasse a dozen feet below. She heard Mary Anne's cries.

And then she heard the buzzing.

Rattlesnakes? In a cave?

She pointed her headlight over the edge and saw Mary Anne's eyes gazing up at her. And she saw the snakes.

Angie said, "They'll be sleepy. Just don't move around, Mary Anne!"

"I'll come down, just be still!" Cameron said.

"No!" cried Mary Anne. As in, *No, you're pregnant!*

It was Angie who insisted on going down, using one of Cameron's hiking poles to move snakes away from Mary Anne so that they could try to move a rock pinning Mary Anne's leg. But Mary Anne said they wouldn't be able to move it.

Cameron and Angie both looked at a rock the size of a trashcan pinning her and agreed they couldn't move it.

Cameron went for help. She ran for the entrance. Mary Anne wouldn't have been there at all but for her; now she was lying in a crevasse with her leg trapped by a boulder, surrounded by rattlesnakes. Outside the cave, she dropped her pack and grabbed her cell phone, then began running down the trail, looking at the mobile's screen for a signal.

She slammed into someone and looked up into the friendly face of Graham Corbett. Out for a hike with his mother.

Instantly, two things occurred to Cameron. One was that Mary Anne was trapped in the cave surrounded by venomous snakes. The second was that Graham had a snake phobia. She blurted out, "Mary Anne's trapped in the cave, but you can't help!" and she ran on. She supposed she could have given Graham more information, but what could he do? His cell phone wouldn't work any better on the trail than hers did, and Cameron *knew* he was pathologically terrified of snakes. Time was of the essence. She didn't know the number of the ranger station. When she got to a place where she had a signal, she would call Paul and let him call the rangers.

She was almost at the parking lot before a signal appeared on the screen, and she punched in her code for Paul's mobile.

"Hello?"

"Paul, it's Cameron." *He knows that, he can see it on his mobile, can see who's calling.* "Mary Anne's trapped in the cave, and there are rattlesnakes down there."

"Rattlesnakes? In a cave?"

She did *not* need male skepticism at the moment. "*Yes!* I saw them. There's a nest, and she's in it, and I think her calf's crushed. I don't know. Please get help. I'm going to call 911. It's Big Jim Cave."

"Right." He hung up, and Cameron felt as though she could breathe. Paul would know what to do and do it. He would assemble the fastest rescue team that could be mustered. She would call for an ambulance now. She punched 911 into her cell phone.

RETURNING TO THE CAVE, Cameron found them all in Boulder Gulch above the crevasse.

Her headlamp shone from Mary Anne's white face and the sweat on her upper lip to Graham Corbett crouched beside her, stroking her hair, making sure she was warm. "Should we elevate her legs?" asked Graham.

"Don't…touch…" Mary Anne whispered.

"Not an unsplinted broken leg," said Cameron. "The paramedics are on their way. Is anyone bitten?"

"No," said Graham, who seemed absolutely uncon-
cerned with the snakes.

"Graham just plucked that boulder right off her,"
Angie said.

That was love for you.

Graham, Cameron could see, was madly in love with
Mary Anne. Cameron no longer wanted Graham—which
surely meant Bridget's potion had worked—but part of
her thought, *Will anyone ever love me that way? Enough
to tread through rattlesnakes to save my life?*

Cameron pushed Graham aside to do a quick check
over Mary Anne to make sure she wasn't bleeding and
that everything possible was being done to prevent her
going into shock. "Paul is getting the rescue team—the
rangers—and the paramedics will be here really soon. If
your leg really hurts—"

"It does," Mary Anne whispered.

"—just try and let go. We'll be quiet. Yell if you need
to. Want a sip of water?"

"Nooo…."

The minutes seemed interminable. Mary Anne had
passed out when Graham moved the boulder and had
come to only after he had got her above the crevasse.
Now, she seemed to swim in and out of consciousness.

This is my best friend, Cameron thought. How could
she ever have let something as stupid as a man come
between them? Why had she ever thought Graham was
so wonderful anyway?

"Were those voices?" Angie said.

Cameron had heard the sounds, too, from the mouth

of the cave. She stood up. "I'll guide them back here. They're here, Mary Anne.

"Back here!" she called and started toward the rescue team.

She met them halfway, and the first face she saw was Paul's, beneath his helmet and headlamp. Relief washed through her. He was so damned competent and reliable. Then, she saw that there were rangers and two paramedics from the ambulance team with him. The ambulance must be here.

They had a backboard with them, and Cameron led the way to where Mary Anne lay. As she watched the paramedics work over her friend, there was a moment when Mary Anne's eyes drifted toward Paul and Cameron, and Cameron knew that Mary Anne was thinking about the pregnancy. Mary Anne knew, and Paul did not. It was wrong.

I've got to tell him.

Paul, however, was watching Graham Corbett crouch beside Mary Anne, holding her hand, and Paul's face showed a mixture of mystified bemusement and hardened cynicism.

The paramedics agreed to immobilize Mary Anne's leg. Angie said she would ride back to town with Graham, and Cameron said she'd meet Graham at the hospital.

Graham was obviously worried about Mary Anne. What Cameron felt surprised her. It seemed childish to wish, at this moment, that Graham would care about her, Cameron, this way. Maybe what she wanted was for *someone* to care about her, but that wasn't it, either. She didn't need a man caring about her to feel valuable within herself.

Perhaps what Bridget had given her *was* what she'd said it was—a specific to restore emotional equilibrium. And maybe it was working. It couldn't be a love potion, in any case.

Why not, Cameron? Surely a potion that made you fall in love with Paul would stop *your being in love with Graham....*

But she wasn't in love with Paul.

She looked toward him. He was taking off his helmet as Cameron slung on her backpack. The others went ahead, following Mary Anne on the backboard, and she and Paul fell in behind them under the gray skies and half-denuded autumn trees, the ground thick with leaves. He said, "Isn't she supposed to be madly in love with Jonathan Hale?"

It was a convoluted story. Mary Anne *had* been madly in love with the manager of the local public radio station, Jonathan Hale. When he became engaged—to Angie Workman, actually—Cameron had suggested that Mary Anne buy one of Clare Cureux's love potions and dose him with it. All in fun, of course. But Graham Corbett had ended up drinking the potion. Then, Jonathan had broken his engagement with Angie anyway—though she seemed to think goodbye and good riddance at this point, which was Cameron's opinion, too. And now Mary Anne was in love with Graham, and he was in love with her. But Cameron couldn't tell Paul all of this, because who had received the love potion was a secret, though he *had* discovered that Mary Anne had bought one.

Not from me, Cameron reminded herself.

"What is it with women?" Paul said, still evidently thinking about Mary Anne, Jonathan Hale and Graham. "Actually—" he glanced warily at Cameron "—that's not what I mean. But this is proof that humans are *not* inherently monogamous."

Any heart, any optimism, Cameron retained after the catastrophic morning seemed to fail her. *I'm capable of monogamy,* she thought. But it didn't matter because the trait wasn't going to be called upon—not by Paul, at any rate.

Starting down the trail ahead of him, she said, "You know, you really might want to talk to someone about your feelings around your parents' divorce."

"Is that what Sean suggests?"

Cameron spun around on the trail, her eyebrows drawing together. Just behind her, Paul stopped. "No. But he *has* had therapy, if you want to know. He's not afraid to talk or to *reveal* his emotions, none of which are shameful characteristics, by the way." *Be calm, Cameron,* she told herself. "I've found out more about what he thinks and feels in a couple of weeks than I've learned about you in years."

Looking skeptical, Paul remarked, "And that makes you want to hitch your cart to his horse."

"No!" she exclaimed. "It's all the same to me, but *you*—in contrast—think 'counseling' is a dirty word. And where has all this manful silence and stoicism gotten you? You have a belief that defies what you see around you. *Many* people marry and stay married. Your parents didn't, and so you assert that nobody can be monogamous, nobody can stay married. Really what you mean is that you personally hate the idea of being tied down."

"No, that is *not* what I mean. And infidelity isn't the only reason people divorce. Look at my parents. They just stopped getting along. That's what they said when my father moved out. 'We're not getting along. We think it will be better this way.' I mean, I was six years old, and I was expected to get along with Bridget. I wasn't given the option of moving out. I thought it would be better if we gave her to a neighbor. But these adults couldn't handle what they demanded of me."

Cameron said, "That's what they told *you.*"

Paul squinted slightly, gazing down at her. But he said nothing, then finally shrugged as though to admit that she might be right.

She turned again and started walking, and Paul wanted to tug on one of her two long, messy braids. He wanted to reach around her and hug her, backpack and all. And he did reach forward, pulling her back against him. He said, "If you were my sister, I wouldn't have wanted to give you away."

Cameron's heart thudded hard in her chest. She looked down and saw one of his big calloused hands. *I can tell him now.* She opened her mouth, and he released her.

She turned to look at him, and his eyes were right on hers.

If she told him, what would he do? Would he marry her out of duty? Or would he simply refuse to marry her?

He said, "You know, they're still friends. I think what

they told me was true. They couldn't live together and get along. It just happens, Cameron. That's with normal people, not men who basically hate women or women who hate men."

"You don't really think I hate men, do you?" she demanded.

"No," he said. "But I sometimes think you want men to act like women. Or you *think* you do."

"What is that supposed to mean?"

"Which part?"

"All of it!"

He seemed to consider something—perhaps the wisdom of answering. He said, "I meant that you say you want men to be more open, to talk about all their interior feelings, to constantly—" he held up fingers to indicate quotations "—'talk things through.' This is the way women behave. It is unnatural to men. Men tend to express emotions in action. But you say you would like to meet a man, maybe have a relationship with a man who bends your ear with blow-by-blow accounts of his inner turmoil. I contend, however, that you would *not* like that."

"Sean's like that!" she exclaimed.

"So hook up with him. He seems willing."

Cameron tried to see if Paul actually hoped she would do this, if Paul actually wanted her to be in a relationship with Sean.

She had her answer in a moment.

He said, "But I don't see you doing that. Have you ever wondered why that is?"

Cameron frowned. Paul was watching her with a look

she caught on his face sometimes. She thought it was affectionate. But she also thought it was like the way she looked at Mariah when she was a puppy. She and Mariah would be at the park, playing on the ice, and Mariah would see another dog and start her bad bitch routine, barking and snarling, and then she'd slip on the ice in the middle of it and fall down.

Cameron wheeled around and started down the trail. She kept talking, not wanting to see his face. "You're saying that I'm not attracted to Sean because he talks to me about his emotions, but that's not it."

Paul made a sound that indicated he was listening.

"There's no chemistry there, that's all."

"There's nothing *unknown* there," Paul answered.

Cameron frowned. "Anyhow, therapy isn't something you do with your partner. A partner isn't a therapist. But everybody can do with figuring out why they are the way they are."

"Presupposing that there's something wrong."

"There's always something wrong," she answered. "We're none of us perfect."

Behind her, Paul wished he could see inside her head. She was nervous. What was going on with Cameron?

"In any case," she continued, "I seriously doubt your parents *just stopped getting along*. Since they obviously do get along to a certain extent."

"But they couldn't live together. My mom loves being a midwife more than anything else. Or anyone."

In front of him, Cameron heard these words and wondered if they were true. She thought they might be.

It was something to think about. Like the way to tell Paul she was pregnant.

But before she did that, she had an appointment with a midwife—and not Clare Cureux.

THE MIDWIFE SHE FOUND was named Beulah Ann Cockburn. Beulah Ann operated out of a clinic in Welch, in McDowell County. When Cameron arrived in her clinic the Monday before Thanksgiving, she discovered that Beulah Ann was a full-bodied blonde around Cameron's own age, perhaps a bit older. She was the divorced mother of two children.

Cameron felt comfortable surrounded by the same sort of handouts and posters available at the Women's Resource Center. She knew most of Beulah Ann's clients were probably low-income and maybe not very well-educated.

After a pregnancy test—*just to double-check*—and a pelvic exam, Beulah Ann sat down with Cameron and looked at her thoughtfully. The midwife was from Louisiana somewhere and still sounded like it. "You're tiny, but your pelvis looks normal to me. This isn't a case of true CPD—cephalopelvic disproportion. Just because you have a sister who had trouble, that doesn't mean that's going to happen to you."

Cameron felt a new ray of hope. It was safe, then, to believe that this pregnancy would go well. In fact, it was imperative to do so, to think positively.

"In fact, I'd suggest you completely forget about the possibility. You should start believing that you can have a healthy pregnancy and a normal vaginal delivery."

"Because if I don't, I will have caused it."

Beulah Ann made a dismissive gesture with her hands. "To be honest, I have more faith in your pelvis than in your ability to make yourself miscarry through worry. Let me give you a list of books to read."

Cameron stopped at a used bookstore on the way home. The only book from Beulah Ann's list that she could find was a very battered copy of *Spiritual Midwifery* by Ina May Gaskin. Cameron was walking to her ancient Datsun when her cell phone rang.

It was the number of the zoo, Paul's work number. She decided to answer.

"Hello?"

"Hi. Want to come to the Last Dollar Saloon tonight? I'm playing."

"No. Too smoky."

"Are you mad at me?" he abruptly asked.

Cameron wondered what the question meant. She'd never known him to ask this before—probably because she usually let him know when she was mad. "No," she answered.

"You have a date with Sean, don't you?"

"I'm not *dating* Sean."

"Does he know that?"

"We're just friends."

"Then, what's wrong? Is this about what hap—"

"No," she cut him off. "Of course not." She wondered what would happen if she told him now that she was pregnant and that she'd just been to see a midwife. Why *wasn't* she telling him now?

Because she knew he wouldn't marry her. She doubted

he would want to commit to her. And she wasn't one hundred percent sure she wanted him to know that she was carrying his child.

"Are you mad because you *want* to be my girlfriend?" he asked.

Cameron's breath caught. She couldn't tell whether he liked this idea or whether he was concerned that she wanted to get her claws into him. "I'm not mad," was what she finally said. *I've got to tell him.*

But Paul would laugh, laugh because she was days pregnant and already knew and was already worried.

"I have something to tell you," she blurted out.

"Did you give me a love potion?" he demanded.

Cameron couldn't help it. She burst out laughing. "Why would I give *you* a love potion?"

Sitting in the primate keeper area, gazing through a reinforced window at the chimpanzees, Paul regretted the question. He spent too much time thinking about Cameron, wondering what it would be like to be… well…to have a different relationship with her.

"Do you feel as though someone has given you a love potion?" Her voice sounded suspicious. "Like you're in love with me or something?"

"No!" This word felt like a lie and a cruelty on his tongue. He almost choked on it. "I mean—I love you," he mumbled stupidly. "You know, in a way. I mean, we're good friends. Where are you, anyhow?" he asked. "The people at the resource center said you took a vacation day."

"Just something I have to do once in a while, especially toward the end of the year, or I lose them, you know."

Paul noticed she didn't say where she actually was. "Okay," he finally said. "We're having a family dinner Friday night. My mother asked me to invite you."

"Sure," she said. Clinging to her cell phone, her eyes suddenly flooding though she didn't understand why, she said, "I'll talk to you later."

My mother asked me to invite you.

Meaning he hadn't thought of it.

Cameron hung up and checked her phone. She had a text message from Sean.

Haiku for C
Fairy-tale princess
Long braids and dark eyes. I'll take
Care of you and baby.

Her throat was dry. She knew Sean and knew that he was offering friendship, would offer more if she wanted it. She wondered how much of her fear of telling Paul had to do with her certainty that he would not be able to vow to do what Sean had just said he would.

All of your fear, Cameron; that's how much.

She texted Sean back.

Haiku for S
Thank you for being
the grown-up you are. We're just
fine, baby and me.

Myrtle Hollow

CAMERON FELT decidedly off. Queasy with the horrible reality that she was pregnant with Paul's child and hadn't yet told him so. The sight of Bridget gutting the last pumpkin of the season nauseated her. Especially as Bridget had paused to discuss love potions with Paul and her father.

Mary Anne and Graham's engagement announcement was in the paper.

Paul said that the love potions clearly didn't work, because Mary Anne had dosed Jonathan Hale with the love potion. This was conjecture on his part and entirely wrong. But Cameron was sworn to secrecy.

Bridget said, "Hey, Cameron, who is that incredible-looking guy I keep seeing you with?"

Paul, Cameron noticed, did not so much as look up, but he said, "I told you who he is, Bridget."

"I'm asking *Cameron.*"

Cameron told her.

"Are you seeing him?" Bridget asked.

"We're just friends."

"Would he like to be more?"

Cameron knew that Sean probably would like to be more, but she didn't want to think about that possibility when Paul didn't even yet know that she was pregnant—pregnant with his child. Suddenly she could no longer remain at the table. She needed to get to the bathroom, and she jumped up and hurried down the narrow hall of the cabin toward Clare Cureux's clean and simple bathroom,

with plants on the windowsill, the walls a sunny yellow.
The house seemed to be tilting back and forth.

She knelt beside the toilet and vomited violently. It
was the worst nausea she'd ever experienced in her life.

"Cameron?"

She'd heard footsteps beside her, and she recognized
Paul's running shoes.

She reached for some toilet paper to wipe her mouth.

"What's wrong?" he asked. "You're sick."

"I'm pregnant," she answered in a hissed exhalation.

CHAPTER FIVE

PREGNANT? "No, you're not," Paul said automatically. No one had slept with Cameron lately but him—he was fairly sure of that—and they had used birth control. But Sean Devlin...

"Oh, yes, I am." She put down the toilet seat cover and rested her arms on it.

Paul stepped into the tiny bathroom far enough to close the door behind him. "Are you serious?"

"I always joke about this."

Paul gazed into her dark brown eyes. To him she looked like some princess of Norse saga. And abruptly, she also looked like a pregnant woman, a mother. *I'm not ready for this.* He decided not to ask if the child was his. Cameron was capable of screaming at him over the question. So he asked, "What are you going to do?"

Cameron sank back on her heels, beyond sobs, beyond tears. "What do you mean?"

He knew he was making all the wrong responses and had no idea what the right responses were. He couldn't stop himself. "Is it mine?"

"You foul—" She swore at him, colorfully and at length.

"I guess that answers my question." Then he said, "Have you seen anyone? A professional? Obstetrician, maybe? You're going to have the baby. I'm reading this right?"

"Don't you think I should?" she demanded.

He realized that he couldn't really imagine her doing anything different. "I'm glad," he said, surprised to find it was true.

Cameron swallowed, relieved and thankful. She searched his face, looking for some sign that he was happy that she was pregnant, that she had become pregnant with this baby that she suddenly wanted desperately to survive. It would be part of Paul and part of her. Being that she *was* pregnant, they seemed to be somewhat on the same page.

Well, that was plenty to be grateful for.

Her mind fought what she was understanding and did not want to understand or know. What she didn't want to be true.

I can't be in love with him.

Being in love with Paul Cureux was a cataclysm.

And it had befallen her.

Paul wavered, uncertain of his role. No, he knew his expected role, but he never did things simply because they were expected or because everyone else did them. Some people—not his parents, his mother, at least—but some other sorts of people would expect him to marry Cameron. Or move in with her. Because she owned her place and it would be absurd for her to move in with him and his housemate, Jake. Or he should buy a house...

A baby.

"So …" He chose his words carefully, finally deciding to repeat his earlier question. "Have you talked to a doctor?"

"A midwife," she said, straightening up and sitting on the edge of the tub. "I've been reading. And, I mean, Paul, your mom's a midwife. The midwife I saw, she said my pelvis is fine. So I want to have a homebirth."

"A *what?*" he said, as though the word was unfamiliar.

"It's better for the baby. You know it is. Of course, I'm terrified, but I want to do it. I want soft lights and the smells of home. I want only the people close to me there—and a trained midwife, of course. I mean, if I have to go to an obstetrician—and to the hospital, for that matter—I'll go. I'm going to do what's best for the baby. Don't doubt that. But for now I've been to a midwife."

Paul leaned back against the door.

Someone knocked on the other side of the wood.

"What?" he said, louder than necessary.

"Just wondering if everything's okay," said Bridget, sounding mischievous. And, to him, extremely nosy.

Paul's eyes narrowed. "Fine," he yelled back. "If we needed your help, we'd have asked for it."

"Pardon me for living," replied his sister, and he listened as her tread receded.

He told Cameron, "She gave you something so you'd get pregnant."

"Your mother and sister don't make such preparations," Cameron retorted. "Stop being paranoid."

"Then she gave you a love potion. That little bottle…"

Cameron felt her face heat. "What makes you think I'm in love with you?"

Paul flushed and changed the subject. "So—home-birth. I might be mistaken, but aren't you the woman who is terrified of pregnancy and giving birth?"

"You need to support me!" she cried. "Of course, I'm scared."

Paul had no wish to support her in insane ideas of homebirth, but he decided to let his mother and father dissuade her. He fully believed in homebirth, knew it was the place for a normal birth. But he wasn't convinced that birth for Cameron would be low-risk.

"Fine," he said and opened the bathroom door. He glanced back to ask, "Shall we tell the family?" He thought that task might be less daunting with her beside him. No one would say anything…unpleasant…with Cameron present.

Cameron nodded. "I guess." She would feel stupid if she miscarried, stupid for letting anyone know that she'd known she was pregnant so early. Before she'd even missed her period.

He waited for her in the hallway, and she wished he would touch her. Reach for her hand. Hug her.

He did neither, simply waited for her to join him.

But in the dimness of the hallway, their eyes met. His lips curved into a smile, and the smile was in his eyes, too, encouragement.

The Cureux family was still assembled in the kitchen, Bridget's preschooler, Nick, standing on a chair to help Clare roll piecrust. Paul's father sat at the table with Bridget's toddler daughter, Merrill, in his lap. Bridget was cleaning up the mess she'd made with the pumpkin.

Clare turned from the counter, looking directly at

Cameron with the dark eyes Paul had inherited. Her long black hair, liberally streaked with gray, hung in two braids which she'd looped up behind her narrow back. Her expression said, *Well?*

Cameron managed a smile. "We're…I'm pregnant."

David's head swung round.

A look of amusement played over Bridget's features. "Congratulations."

Clare said, "Yes," and looked at her son.

So did his father.

Paul said, "Thank you," answering the unasked question and hoping no one would say it out loud.

"Have you seen anyone?" asked Clare and set Nick on the floor. "We'll get back to the pie in a minute," she told him.

Bridget took her squirming daughter from her father's arms.

"Beulah Ann Cockburn, in McDowell County."

"She's good," Clare said approvingly.

"But, as I told her—" Cameron felt a slight fear as she gazed at Paul's strong mother, the formidable woman whom she knew to be the most experienced midwife in the state "—I'd prefer to have you."

Clare nodded. "We'll see."

Cameron felt a resurgence of terror that was too common since her first visit to a midwife. Different terrors. First, that she wouldn't be able to deliver a viable child, that she wouldn't be able to carry the baby long enough. And a second, far lesser, fear—that she would be forced to have a hospital birth and a cesarean.

Granted, a hospital birth would certainly be less painful, and *that* thought tempted her like heroin must send its siren song to a junkie.

But she'd begun reading the books Beulah Ann had recommended and others she'd read about and ordered from Amazon. Natural birth was better for the baby—and ultimately for her. If it was safe, if she could do it.

But Clare knew Cameron's family history—Beatrice's miscarriages and agonizing labor. That had been the meaning of her "We'll see."

Clare was not a woman for embraces and she did not attempt to embrace Cameron, did not even approach her.

But Paul's father stood up, came to her and hugged her briefly. "That's wonderful news," he said. "And did your midwife give you a due date?'

"July twenty-eighth," Cameron told him.

Clare nodded thoughtfully. "Well, let me finish this pie and—we'll make an appointment."

Cameron was disappointed; she'd been hoping Clare would be able to examine her that minute. She wanted to know if Clare agreed with Beulah Ann that Cameron should be able to birth the child vaginally. Well, if she couldn't, then she couldn't.

The melody of "Narcolepsy Baby" by Rhesus rang into the room. Paul's cell phone. He took it from his waist and did touch Cameron then, squeezing her arm before he stepped around the table and went outside.

Cameron had no curiosity about his phone call and knew that he'd gone outside because he didn't want the call to interrupt his family. She wished he'd stayed.

Clare said, "You know that neither Beulah Ann nor I have hospital privileges at this time."

Cameron nodded. She felt exposed. Paul's mother was so strong, so capable, and Cameron knew that she would keep Cameron and the baby safe if it was within her power. Yet she was also strangely pitiless. She was not weak, and Cameron sometimes wondered if she despised weakness in others. But no, that wasn't precisely it. She reminded Cameron of a raven, sitting wise and separate.

Paul came back inside. "A problem at the zoo." He looked at Cameron. "Want to come with me?"

Grateful, she caught up her coat from where it lay on a bench against the wall and followed Paul out the door.

PAUL NEVER TALKED on the phone and drove at the same time, so he handed the keys to his truck to Cameron.

In his ear, Helena Ruffles said, "I don't know how it happened. And Portia's the only one I saw."

The graduate student had returned to the zoo at dusk and seen Portia sitting on a bench outside the saki exhibit, looking in at the sakis. She had immediately returned to the parking lot, gotten in her car, and called Paul.

"Are you sure it was Portia?"

"Definitely." Helena knew Portia better than anyone. But Portia was a wild animal, a chimpanzee, inhumanly strong and inherently unpredictable.

"Stay in your car. If you see any others, be prepared to drive away if they notice your car. I'm on my way and making some calls. Then I'll call you back."

"I don't want anyone to do anything that will set us back!" Helena begged.

And Paul understood. He had held Portia when she was younger. But now she weighed a hundred and thirty-five pounds and could rip apart the iron fence surrounding the zoo if she chose. And after this incident, no matter its outcome, they would have to reevaluate the safety and wisdom of continuing Helena's research.

Suddenly, Paul wished Cameron wasn't with him. She would have to remain in the truck in the parking lot with the doors locked. Portia was unlikely to approach the truck for any reason, but if she did…

A weight of responsibility surrounded him. He would deal with Cameron in a moment. But he had more calls to make first.

His next call was to the zoo director, Samuel Bannister, PhD.

"Hello?" answered a woman's voice as Cameron steered the truck out of Myrtle Hollow and toward the shortest route to the main road.

"This is Paul Cureux. Is Dr. Bannister there?" Paul disliked the former sociology researcher's insistence on the honorific and refusal to let underlings use his Christian name, but now was not the time to push anyone. "It's about the zoo."

"Well, he's busy just now."

"It's an emergency."

"Well. I'll see."

Looking anxious, Cameron picked her way along the road, slowing as the headlights caught a deer.

"Paul?" The director's voice.

Thank God.

"Portia's out."

"How did *that* happen?"

"No one knows yet. We need the vet and the shooting team until the vet arrives. Will you call Dr. Marshall? I'll round up the other guys."

"I hope you don't have to shoot her."

"Me, too." Paul thought his heart would break if someone shot the chimpanzee. He loved her above all the other animals at the zoo. But if Portia could not be subdued with a tranquilizer gun or otherwise persuaded back into her enclosure, she would have to be shot. Though the zoo was closed, it was evening and if Portia escaped the park there was a threat to the public. Paul had an inner damn-the-public feeling, but he was a strong believer in following protocol—and he well knew that an escaped great ape could pose a threat to the public. Still, while not freezing, it was cold. Surely they wouldn't stray too far from their home.

Don't leave the zoo, Portia. Don't leave the zoo.

If she really wouldn't cooperate, then George Marshall could get her with the tranquilizer gun.

Paul quickly called the two other members of the zoo's shooting team, then closed his phone. "Okay, pull over at the gas station up there."

"You want to drive?" Cameron asked.

"No, I want to leave you there."

"You invited me to come!"

"I wasn't thinking. I'm sorry. I'll come back for you.

I don't have time to take you home, but I don't want you out there at the zoo."

The gas station was closed, and Cameron said, "It's cold, and there's nobody around. I don't want to be left here."

"Keep driving, then." He would find somewhere else to leave her. "Look, Portia's a wild animal, and this is a dangerous situation. All right. You're going to drive me there, let me out, lock the doors and drive back to the *park* entrance." Which was a good five miles from the zoo. "I will phone you when it's okay to come back."

"Why can't I sit in the parking lot in the truck?"

Paul had seen *after* photos of two people who'd been mauled by chimps—both male chimps, both kept as pets. He said, "Cameron, *please*." He didn't sound like himself. What was this? All these feelings.

He was worried about Portia. That was it. That *must* be it.

Protocol. Return to protocol.

And protocol's place for a pregnant Cameron McAllister was the park entrance.

Paul talked on the phone to Helena through the rest of the ride to the zoo's employee entrance. At least it was Portia and not one of the males, he and Helena told each other over and over. But what if the males were out, too?

Paul was attached to all the zoo's primates—and many of the other animals—but he'd often wished for orangutans or gorillas over chimpanzees. Of course, that might be because he'd had no experience with the former. He had met a couple in Morgantown that kept a chimp as a pet—in fact, he'd met the animal. The situation appalled him, and he'd told the owners so and told them why. *These are animals. These are very strong animals. These animals can and will injure or kill you.* The couple had told him that the chimp was like a son to them.

God. *People.*

Portia's situation was different. She was a zoo animal, and Helena was doing research on language with no harm to Portia and with constant attention to safety. Helena was trying to determine if chimps would ever use language to communicate for the sake of communication rather than simply *aping* what they had learned in order to receive a reward. Most research to date had supported the latter probability.

Paul's view was that chimps chose to do what they wanted to do and what they wanted to do was seldom the equivalent of sitting around philosophizing.

Closing his phone, Paul climbed out of the truck beside Helena's car. "Lock the doors and go," he told Cameron. As she drove away, a sedan pulled up and parked, and another keeper, Aron from Reptiles, stepped out with his rifle. Paul's rifle was inside the zoo. Helena got out of her car.

They stood in the parking lot, carefully scanning the area, especially the trees within the zoo, and waited for the others.

"If Portia's out, the others must be, too," Aron remarked.

Paul presumed that was the case. His assistant keeper had been the one to give the chimps their vitamins that afternoon and hence the last one to secure their enclosure. And by that time Paul had left for a meeting with the local SPCA who had rescued a macaque from a local home. The animal was malnourished and had injured one of its owners, and Paul could not say if the zoo would be able to take the animal. Paul had advised the SPCA on housing for the animal. In West Virginia, you could keep almost anything as a pet.

The vet showed up with his tranquilizer gun and another keeper with a rifle.

Outdoor lights on, into the zoo through the employee entrance, weapons ready, everyone looking out for escaped chimps. Paul heard laughterlike vocalizations from farther in the park and looked ahead to see two chimps wrestling and rolling on the grass, while another had knocked over a popcorn vendor's wagon and was throwing popcorn kernels at the rhinos.

This chimp saw Paul and screamed.

The keepers and vet ran back to the entrance and back out, and the chimp reached the bars and screamed at them until the vet darted him. Then he ran off, or began to, moving drunkenly in midstride. The vet efficiently reloaded. Paul knew it would be a miracle if all the chimps survived this disaster. Aron jumped in his vehicle and drove around to the front of the zoo to make sure none of the chimps escaped that way. All five must be out. Thank God Helena hadn't been hurt.

The fire department arrived with a firehose Paul had requested, and he was able to use the hose to direct Portia and Anthony, the youngest male, back into their area, while the vet darted another male. The last of the group climbed on top of the Big Cat House and began pulling tiles from the roof and throwing them. The vet darted him, as well.

The weakness in the enclosure was discovered when Paul attempted to lock Anthony and Portia inside. The steel door frame was missing, the chimps having used their strong nails to pry loose fittings and unscrew bolts. Paul blamed himself, because he had felt something different in the door and had not investigated thoroughly enough.

The animals were all temporarily housed in holding cages in the zoo's animal hospital, and Paul was in the chimp exhibit investigating damage when Cameron walked in.

"What are you doing here?" he said. "I told you to stay at—"

"You didn't call, and I threw up again, so I came back, and the firemen told me all the chimps were put away."

Paul said, "Do you know what they can do to people?"

"I was the one locked securely in your truck."

"They can pull the doors off that truck." He grabbed Cameron's arm and marched her outside into the night lights of the zoo, where he showed her the bench one of the chimps had ripped out of the concrete.

Cameron started shaking and then had to kneel beside the duck pond to throw up again. "What were you doing with them, then?" she shouted.

"Getting them contained. It's my job. We had rifles, a dart gun and a firehose. Why didn't you call?"

"My phone's dead, and your charger wasn't in the truck."

"It's under the seat. You look green."

"Of course I do."

Paul tried to remember anything his mother had said about what to do for morning sickness. He seemed to recall that protein was involved, and this made sense to him from his observations of the zoo's primates. "Come with me."

He led the way into the keeper area. He had an irrational desire to check every enclosure in the zoo to make sure no animals were out who could injure Cameron. He'd never felt that way before, but the chimps' escape had unsettled him.

He indicated the bench near the lockers, and while she sat, he stepped into the small kitchen, opened the refrigerator and brought out cheese. He sliced cheese, brought crackers from the cupboard and added some baby carrots. He brought her the plate, then said, "I've got to look at the chimps."

"Isn't the vet with them?"

"Yes, but they're my responsibility." What he didn't want to say was that he needed to reaffirm for himself that the chimps actually were in the cages. He feared he would have nightmares about a chimp attacking Cameron.

She's pregnant. I'm going to be a father.

The last thought was too overwhelming—too new and strange—to be long contemplated, not when there were other things to do. He never wanted to be so much as a pet owner. He liked children well enough but knew their propensity for entirely reorganizing their parents' lives. Well, he supposed he'd have to be some kind of part-time father.

He didn't like that thought. Kids deserved full-time parents. Of course, *he'd* had a part-time father. Parents worked part of the time, in any case.

Only Portia and Anthony, who had been only lightly sedated for the move, were stirring. Paul approached Portia's cage, and she reached through the bars and lightly stroked his fingers. He touched her rough fingers in return. "Sorry for all the excitement, Portia. I don't suppose you want to say who pulled up the bench." He wished Helena was there to ask Portia this in sign language, which Portia knew.

George Marshall sat at his desk at the hospital, apparently updating patient charts. Besides the chimps, the only other inmates were a serval, a wild-caught copperhead in quarantine and awaiting tick removal before moving to her new exhibit, and a ring-tailed lemur who was Paul's charge and unusually susceptible to parasites.

"How is he?" he asked George, pausing at the lemur's cage and watching the round brown eyes that gazed back at him.

"Same old, same old." George stood up. "And if you put him back in with the rest of them, he's going to spread it again."

"Maybe he's not getting rid of it the first time," Paul suggested.

"It's occurred to me. I recommend an extended time on his own."

"They hate that," Paul said. The lemurs loved being together. It was the nature of lemurs.

"He's doing all right. When the chimps are out of here and we can have small school groups through here again, he'll get visitors. He likes that."

The door of the infirmary opened, and Cameron came in, looking much better.

"Stay away from the cages," Paul said. He had given Anthony plenty of room, only allowing Portia to touch him.

"Which one's Portia?" she asked, her eyebrows drawing together.

Paul nodded toward the female's cage.

Portia sat down in her cage and glanced at Cameron from the corner of her eye. She wasn't always friendly, and she didn't know Cameron. Cameron had seen Portia before but couldn't tell the chimps apart.

Cameron surveyed the slumbering apes.

"They'll all have hangovers," George remarked.

"Did they have a good time?" asked Cameron, who knew the veterinarian.

"Probably," George admitted.

The door opened again, and the zoo director walked in. *Finally,* Paul thought. *Dr.* Bannister should have shown his face a half hour earlier to help make the hard decisions.

"Are they all right? How did they get out?" the zoo director demanded.

Paul said, "Come on. I'll show you. Cameron, stay away from the cages. *All* the cages."

As they stepped out of the infirmary, the zoo director informed him of the liability issues of having a nonemployee in the infirmary while not on a guided tour. Paul took him to the chimp exhibit, and when the director saw the damage, he almost rubbed his hands together gleefully.

"This," he said, "is the fault of the designer of the exhibit. He's to blame. He'll have to correct the flaws."

Paul remained silent, thankful for the first time in his life for the director's single-minded obsession with looking for blame outside of his own realm.

Dr. Bannister looked at him. "Is that girl a family member?"

"Uh…yes," Paul said finally. "In a way."

The zoo director, vaguely concerned about liability, heard only the part of the answer that he wanted to hear.

"THERE WILL STILL be food," Paul said, driving out of the park at eleven. "At my mother's house. She went to bed, but she said we can help ourselves."

Cameron could barely keep her eyes open. "I'll just go home."

Paul felt responsible for her not eating. She'd eaten cheese and crackers at the zoo, but she needed a real meal. "I'll cook for you at your house."

"I just want to sleep."

"I think it's not eating that causes morning sickness."

"No, I need protein and B6," she said matter-of-factly. She'd read about morning sickness. "And no stress," she added.

"Find a new job," he muttered.

"Ha ha. I got to touch fingers with Portia. George said it was all right."

Paul wanted to murder the veterinarian.

He pulled the truck over and put it in neutral. "She could have grabbed your arm and bitten it off! You think I'm kidding? You know what it looks like when they attack people? She is not a *pet*. Helena doesn't even sit in the same room with her to do her research!"

"You're overreacting. I've seen pictures of Dian Fossey sitting with gorillas in the wild."

"Portia is not a gorilla, and *I* wouldn't sit around with gorillas in the wild. They're wild animals. I love them! Never go near any of the chimps again! They can kill you. In the wild, they kill their infants and eat them."

Realizing what he'd just said, he put his hand over his face. "I'm sorry," he said.

Cameron, however, seemed unfazed. "George wouldn't have let me if it wasn't safe."

"It *wasn't* safe, and he *did* let you."

"He was standing right there."

I could kill him, Paul thought again.

"Their teeth are sharp as knives. *Promise me,*" he said, "you will not do anything like that again."

"Why do you care?" she asked, half fishing for information on his feelings for her, half-disgusted at what appeared to be a chauvinistic response to having conceived a child.

"I like you!" he almost shouted. "Your pretty face is part of my life! And I don't want chimpanzees killing you, all right? You're my friend."

Cameron noticed that he didn't mention that she was pregnant. She considered turning him loose in her kitchen. He would make a mess. He and Jake were slobs. She would wake up in the morning to a horrible mess.

"I won't be awake to eat any food anyhow," she said.

He put the car in gear. At her house, he turned off the engine and got out.

There was a greeting-card-size envelope on her front door with her name on it, and nearby, leaning against the outside of the cabin, was a Christmas wreath. The card was from Sean, and it showed a picture of two puppies playing together on the front. Inside, he'd written, *To brighten your season. Your friend, Sean.*

Paul perused the card over her shoulder. He picked up the wreath. "I'll hang it up for you." He'd have preferred to throw it in the river but recognized this response as childish.

"Thank you." Cameron let him follow her into the house, where she dropped the card on her entry table. She found she was trembling. Would he want to make love with her? Was he suddenly interested in her because of their child?

She was too exhausted to figure it out. Wolfie looked at them, and Mariah followed them inside.

Paul said, "Go to sleep. I'll wake you when the food is ready."

Cameron thought, *This is scary,* and she wasn't thinking about his wreaking havoc in her kitchen. What frightened her was that she knew herself to be in love with him. And she was afraid he would *think* he loved her back, think so and then change his mind.

That she would grow used to his presence and his kind treatment of her, and then, one way or another, he would abandon her and their child.

Myrtle Hollow

CLARE HAD NOT gone right to bed, because her ex-husband had not left. She knew he'd deliberately stayed till after Bridget and her children had departed, and Clare knew why.

Bridget and the kids drove away.

David said, "So."

"Yes," Clare replied. Both of them thinking of Paul and Cameron.

"The man who doesn't want so much as a houseplant."

"I don't expect he'll marry her," Clare said wearily. It seemed sad to acknowledge this of her own son, but she couldn't imagine Paul committing himself to marriage.

"I expect he better," David said grimly.

"If you think he will, you don't know your own son."

"What I don't know about my son," he replied, "is the reason for this nonsense he has about never being married. It's time for him to grow up."

"He is grown-up. He simply believes that no one can remain monogamous."

"He's not that illogical. He believes *he* can't," her ex-husband replied. "And *I* think you have something to tell him, Clare."

"It has nothing to do with Paul. If you think he needs to know," she challenged, "*you* tell him." She knew David never would. He considered the business shameful to her and would not reveal her shame to their children. It really wasn't their business anyhow. It was hers and David's.

"You know full well I'll never tell him," David answered.

"We decided decades ago what we would tell them, and that's what we told them."

To her surprise, he said, "I think you're right. I'm looking for excuses for his being the way he is, and there really *is* no excuse."

"*I'm* certainly not to blame," Clare said. "He's an adult. Whatever his problems are, he needs to get over them and stop blaming his parents."

"He doesn't blame us," David said, "because he doesn't see a problem with the way he is. He wants to remain single and considers it his right. But I hope he understands now that he has somewhat abridged that right."

"I don't see that," Clare replied. "This isn't the 1950s, when a man was expected to marry a girl he'd 'gotten in trouble.'" She used the expression ironically.

"Yes," David agreed. "Never have adults had more support in bad behavior, more freedom to be selfish."

His sidelong look at Clare silently accused, and she accepted the accusation. "Call it selfishness," she said. "I did what I had to. I did what I *wanted*, but it was also what I needed."

Her ex-husband pushed back from the table, rose and slowly reached for his coat.

They had reached the topic on which they had never agreed and never would, and so he was leaving.

Just as he had twenty-five years before.

CHAPTER SIX

PAUL FOUND defrosted chicken in her refrigerator, along with red bell peppers and other vegetables. He put rice on the stove and walked to the bedroom doorway. Cameron lay on top of the covers, fully clothed and obviously asleep. The sight stirred him. He remembered her full breasts as he'd seen them the night they'd made love.

It had been very good—all of it.

And now she's pregnant, Paul.

It must be his sister's work, Bridget's witchery. Not the pregnancy—not that. And obviously, he had a responsibility in going to bed with Cameron. But it was unlike Cameron to have accepted his…suggestion. And Bridget *was* untrustworthy.

He hadn't the slightest idea what he would do with a baby and had an unsettling remembrance of caring for a six-week-old Nicky for Bridget and her husband. Nicky had been unwilling to drink from a bottle. He had screamed, peed and defecated. But Paul had liked him even then. He had smelled so good, that baby smell.

Cameron's going to have a baby.

In his mind, he kept trying to separate the fact that it was

Cameron's baby from the fact that it was his baby. Babies were something he could take care of for a few hours. They weren't something to have around all the time, in a car seat, in the backseat where an air bag could not kill them, with a bag full of their paraphernalia. No night gigs, no dinners at restaurants, no morning runs, no *freedom.* They were a massive imposition on freedom, and Paul chafed at the thought of the being he felt thrust upon him.

But now that Cameron was pregnant, the baby seemed a *fact.* He would have to have something to do with it. It just wasn't an option to have nothing to do with his child. Kids needed dads.

They need full-time dads, Paul.

Well, *he* hadn't exactly had a full-time dad. His father had walked out when he was six. And while Paul had still seen lots of him, always, while his dad was still there for Little League games, while he'd slept over at his father's house almost half of each week, well, David Cureux had still not been a full-time dad.

And Paul still resented it, if he let himself think about it. It wasn't his nature to dwell on such things, and a quick sight of Cameron's dressing table gave him something different to think about. Sean Devlin's self-published poetry volume.

Paul picked it up. Followed by Mariah as he returned to the kitchen to slice vegetables, he opened the chapbook and read a poem. Dark, brooding stuff. It ended with the line, *I called, and you did not come.*

It was about abandonment, and Paul reminded himself that he was fortunate to have had two parents, to have grown up near both, to have always been treated well by both. If he had called, someone had always come.

The thought of being a part-time father left him with the same feeling as imagining neglecting any of his charges at the zoo. A dirty exhibit, bored monkeys... It was the same feeling. At the zoo, he never let such things happen.

But he was considering being a part-time dad.

Well, he *could* take care of the child now by taking care of Cameron. Physically. Making sure she ate. And went to an obstetrician, for God's sake. *A homebirth?* What was she thinking? He couldn't imagine a baby's head passing through her pelvis.

Well, his mother was a realist. She'd seen enough as a midwife that she had no patience with fantasists. Women with unrealistic expectations were set right. And Paul had no doubt his mother would set Cameron straight.

He remembered Cameron, rather recently, talking about miscarriages—her sister having had a string of miscarriages. He saw now why she'd become hysterical on the subject. She'd believed—or known—that she was pregnant. To him, too, the prospect of a miscarriage was nightmarish—after the things Cameron had said. Because it would hurt *her.* That would be the nightmare.

Mariah kept him company, gladly accepting scraps, as he stood at the stove.

When the meal was ready, he dished up two plates, carried both into the bedroom, and set them on the bed. He switched on a bedside lamp.

Cameron didn't stir, and he said, "Hey."

Nothing.

He touched her arm, felt her warmth through the soft cotton of her long-sleeve T-shirt.

She blinked, and her dark brown eyes focused on him, adjusting to the light.

He propped two pillows against the headboard for her and gestured to the plates beside her.

She sat up, her braids mussed, and it occurred to him that she was the most beautiful woman he knew. And she was pregnant with his child. She was the only woman he would want carrying his child, that was certain.

Though, of course, he didn't precisely *want* a child. Nor did he *not want* this child.

He sat cross-legged on the bed to eat and to make sure she ate.

She said, "Thank you." Then, "It's good."

When she was done eating, she got up and carried her plate to the kitchen. He followed with his own plate and saw her look around at the mess. He saw her accept that she was too tired to clean up. In resignation, she headed back toward the bathroom. He decided to wash dishes, cutting down the work by first offering them to Mariah and Wolfie, then filling the sink with soapy water and finishing the job properly.

When he was done, he returned to the bedroom and found that Cameron had changed into a T-shirt and sweatpants, brushed her teeth probably, and was asleep. It was unlike her. She was an energetic woman, liking to oversee everything in her home.

Her exhaustion impressed upon him again that this was real, that she was pregnant.

Pregnant with his child.

He wanted nothing so much as to climb into bed with her, but he hadn't been invited. Besides, it might…complicate matters. If he behaved as a partner to her, as a lover now, she might draw mistaken conclusions about his long-term intentions.

Until he knew what those intentions were, it would be better if she drew no conclusions.

He let himself out of her house and suddenly felt exhausted. Part of him kept screaming, *This isn't what I wanted. This isn't what I planned!*

CAMERON'S INITIAL prenatal visit with Clare Cureux was punctuated by episodes of vomiting. Clare gave her vitamin B6 from her own cabinet and encouraged her to eat more protein.

Lying weakly on the four-poster bed Clare used for exams, Cameron wondered if she'd been smart to ask Clare to be her care provider. Normally, the father of her child should be present at a prenatal exam, but Paul had shown no interest, except to say, "When you go to her backup physician, I'll come with you." Cameron had seen this as Paul's subtle way of suggesting that their baby should be born in a hospital.

Cameron wanted a homebirth. Only if it was safe, of course. She asked Clare, "Can I do this?"

"Your pelvis is perfectly normal," Clare said. "Barring an exceptionally large baby or something else untoward, I foresee no problem with a vaginal delivery."

"And a homebirth?"

"As far as I know at this point. We'll have to see how things go."

Cameron felt a moment's relief at this moderate reply, then recurring fear of the pain she suspected would be a huge part of the childbirth process. If nothing else stood in the way, her ability to have a natural birth would all be a matter of how much pain she could stand.

"What are you thinking?" Clare demanded perspicaciously.

"I just hope I can…tough it out."

"One thing I guarantee," Clare told her, "nothing anyone tells you will allow you to know what it's like until you do it. The women who have the worst time are the one's who get attached to a particular way of doing things."

"Oh." Cameron wondered if she was like that and decided she had the potential to be.

Cameron wished it could be comfortable to discuss with Clare the simple fact of Paul as a father, but there was no way.

If Clare brought it up, it would be bad enough. But Clare would never bring it up. She undoubtedly saw the situation as Paul and Cameron's problem, or business, at any rate. Which it was.

Clare moved on to the need for Cameron to make an appointment with Clare's backup physician. Cameron was also reassured by this plan. Hopefully, it would ease Paul's reservations, as well. If the physician felt a home-birth would be safe for her, Paul must agree.

As Cameron was walking out of the cabin to her bicycle, her cell phone rang. Paul.

Her heart sped up. She reminded herself, *He's calling because he cares about the baby.*

Not because he feels romantically toward you, Cameron.

She answered.

He said, "I left my iPod at your house."

"I found it. With your wallet. In the kitchen."

"You've had the charge of my wallet all this time?"

"Yes, and I've been using your credit cards."

"Just what I expected of you."

"Thank you for feeding me last night." Abruptly, she changed the subject. "Your mother says a homebirth is safe. Well, so far, she thinks that. She seems to have a conservative attitude. Wait and see."

Paul walked through the animal hospital. Paced, actually, back and forth, occasionally glancing at his charges, none of whom seemed the worse for wear from the previous night's adventure but who would have to be rehoused soon. Repairs on their exhibit were underway. He couldn't believe what he was hearing. "Cameron, you are terrified of childbirth."

"I can't think about that," she said. "I can't think about it or I'll go mad, and I can't let it dictate my decisions. Most women who are unfamiliar with childbirth are frightened. In our culture, childbirth is portrayed as dangerous and painful."

"This might be a good time to let fear have a say." *I'm afraid,* he realized. He knew better than to tell her that.

Paul reasoned with himself that the reality of childbirth would change Cameron. She would go to the hospital.

She said, "Why are you against my having a home-birth? Your mother is a midwife, for heaven's sake."

Maybe that *is* why, Paul thought. His current emotions were irrational. He knew the figures from the births his mother had attended. Two stillbirths, neither of which could or would have been prevented in the hospital, maybe a dozen hospital transports. Of course, there had been that one time, the birth no one would discuss, before his parents' divorce....

On that recent night when he'd asked his parents to relate the incident, no one had obliged.

He spoke as honestly as he could. "A little different reactions come up when it's happening to you. I mean, me. The baby. When a person is involved."

"When, in human childbirth, *isn't* a person involved?" she asked. "Or are you drawing a comparison with pri-mate childbirth?"

"A child that you and I conceived," he said bluntly. "My offspring. It's personal."

Cameron wasn't sure she'd ever heard anyone speak those words so unemotionally. "You're closing yourself off," she remarked. "You're trying not to feel."

He spoke to someone in the background, saying, "I know. I haven't been able to get him to stop."

She heard the person say something in response.

Then, Paul said to Cameron, "You were saying?"

"Nothing. Are you really coming to the doctor with me?"

"Oh, yes." Paul's certainty surprised him.

"Don't think *you're* going to make the decisions." In

Clare's yard, preparing to mount her bicycle, Cameron said the words that were inside her, with her, at every moment. "You don't even know what part you want to have in the baby's life."

The words shocked Paul. Not because of the truth of them but because the truth sounded terrible when articulated. He said, "Let's go out to dinner tonight. My treat."

"I'm incredibly nauseated." Why did he want to take her out to dinner? He never took her out to dinner, and when they happened to eat out at the same place and the same time, they went Dutch. Well, except on those occasions when she was posing as his girlfriend. He'd fed her on the way to and from the Crawl gig. "Well, all right," she said.

"Rick's," he said, naming the best restaurant in Logan.

"I hope I can eat," she said, though the very thought was disgusting.

"Why do you think I'm taking you out now?" he said. "You'll be a cheap date."

MARY ANNE LOOKED a little worse for the wear, Cameron decided when her cousin stopped at the Women's Resource Center late that afternoon. She still wore a cast from the surgery on her leg following her caving accident. In general, Cameron envied Mary Anne's height, the always-smooth look of her honey-colored hair, her style. But it was hard to look stylish on crutches. Cameron, exhausted from reading three grant proposals before their submission, nonetheless jumped up to pull out the most comfortable guest chair in her office for her cousin.

Mary Anne carefully settled into it, then looked up, almost nervously, at Cameron. "Are you still mad?" she inquired.

"About what?" Cameron furrowed her brow.

"About Graham, of course."

While Cameron had certainly not forgotten that she'd ever cared for Graham Corbett or ever been devastated by his love for Mary Anne, other thoughts and feelings had been getting more play recently. "I was never *mad*."

"You were," Mary Anne retorted.

"Maybe a little. But it was never your fault. It was always my problem. And I have other things on my mind right now." She studied Mary Anne. "I'm being taken out to dinner tonight. Could you help me dress?"

"I think so. I'm getting better at steps, and there are fewer up to your house than at Graham's or Nanna's." Nanna was Jacqueline Billingham, their grandmother, with whom Mary Anne still, nominally, lived. The reference to "Graham's" gave lie to that, and Cameron couldn't quite repress a tiny sting of envy. But she thought it was the envy of Mary Anne's knack for doing everything in the right order. Fall in love, get engaged, get married, *then* get pregnant.

Cameron had somehow become pregnant completely out of order.

Her cousin asked, "Who's the lucky man?"

Cameron wondered if pregnancy made a person overheated. Her face felt too warm. "It's just Paul. Don't make a deal about it. "

"The father of your child?" Mary Anne said, as though clarifying matters.

"Undoubtedly that is why he has asked me on a date." For a moment, Cameron considered the timing of his invitation to dinner. He'd asked her immediately after she'd mentioned that she had no idea what role he intended to play in their child's life. She confessed this to her cousin.

"Rick's? He's suddenly taking you to Rick's?" Mary Anne exclaimed. "Obviously he's going to propose!"

Cameron wondered if being engaged herself had addled Mary Anne's wits. "Not a chance," she answered. "This is Paul, remember?" But, whispered a small voice inside her, say he *did* propose. What, then, would she say?

Well, yes, of course.

At least she thought so. If he didn't seem as though he felt obligated to marry her. But Paul virtually never felt obligated to do anything, as far as she could tell. Nothing imposed by societal expectations, anyway.

"He won't ask me to marry him. It's against his philosophy." And she would *not* get her hopes up.

"Men change suddenly," Mary Anne said with the voice of experience.

"I haven't noticed Paul changing, except that he seems to want to push me around." She told Mary Anne of the chimpanzee escape and Paul's treatment of her during and after the episode. Then she related Paul's sudden antipathy toward homebirth.

"He's just being protective," said Mary Anne. "*You* can't want a homebirth, can you? It seems to me that pain control isn't an option."

"That's not the most important thing. Anyhow, I'm not wedded to the idea; it's just my first choice. Hospitals aren't very supportive of women with long labors, for instance. If I go to the hospital, I'm afraid I'll end up having a C-section."

"And the problem with that is?"

"There's no problem, if I *need* one. But I don't want an unnecessary cesarean. If it's unnecessary, it's worse for the baby and worse for me. And if it's safe for the baby, I *want* to experience vaginal delivery."

Mary Anne frowned, her gaze steady and compassionate. "I can understand that." Then she assumed a knowing expression, which Cameron didn't like. "So Paul's a little overprotective. But you say nothing is different between the two of you. Do you want his attitude toward you to be different from what it has been?"

"Of course not. Which is fortunate, because it isn't."

"So how was this child conceived?" Mary Anne inquired.

Flushing when she remembered that the stated purpose of that night together had been to help Cameron get over Graham, Cameron snapped, "It just *happened.* Do you want to help me figure out what to wear or not?"

"Of course, I'll help," Mary Anne replied as Cameron heard the bell that meant someone else had come in.

"Hello?" called a male voice, one Cameron recognized.

Cameron stood, and stepped around Mary Anne to look out the door. "We're in here."

It was Sean, and he came to the open door of the office and handed her an envelope. "Your comp ticket to the high school play. *The Night of January 16th*, by Ayn Rand."

"Thank you!" she said and impulsively hugged him, then turned to introduce Mary Anne. Her cousin, still seated, gazed up at Sean as though someone had just struck her with an unabridged dictionary and Cameron knew she was thinking, *Who is that gorgeous man?*

"I would have gotten you two tickets," he said, "but we're almost sold out."

"Thank you," she repeated. "This is great."

"Have you eaten?" he asked.

"Actually, Paul's taking me to Rick's."

Sean raised his attractively arched eyebrows and smiled. "I wasn't going to propose anything so grand. Just wanted to make sure you got something good."

"Thank you," Cameron said, feeling like a broken record. She emphasized, "Really, I'm doing a good job of that."

"Don't make me feel unnecessary," he answered, showing his dimples.

A trickle of uneasiness went through Cameron. She'd told him about her mixed feelings toward Paul, had even told Sean of what had happened between them back in university days. She tried to be absolutely straight with Sean, but she knew he was attracted to her. And she had told him that she regarded him as a friend, no more.

But should she be more discouraging?

When he left them, after saying it was nice to meet Mary Anne and promising to call Cameron the next day and saying he would take her for dinner the night of the play, Cameron sat back down and Mary Anne said in a low awestruck voice, "My God. That is possibly the best-looking man I've ever seen. And he acts like a lovesick puppy around you. He's in love with you, isn't he?"

"Maybe a little, but it's not mutual, and I've told him so. Anyhow, I have too much on my plate right now. I don't have time for…that," she concluded vaguely.

Now, Mary Anne stared at her in amazement.

Cameron expected her cousin to comment on her idiocy.

Instead, Mary Anne said, "You're in love with Paul, aren't you? Oh, Cameron, be sensible!"

"I can't help what I feel!"

Mary Anne muttered, "If there was ever a time for a love potion—"

"No!" Cameron almost shouted.

"Why not? You persuaded me to buy one."

"That was different. That was just Jonathan Hale, even if Graham did drink it. This time—well, there's another life involved. His father's attachment to his mother shouldn't be based on something as flimsy as a love potion."

Realizing what she *hadn't* said, Cameron blushed and quickly added, "Or mother's to father, for that matter." Pretending that a love potion was needed. Then remembering, belatedly, that she half suspected Bridget of having given her one.

CHAPTER SEVEN

RICK'S WAS UNUSUALLY BUSY that night, with a crowd in the foyer and every bench seat taken. Cameron felt so exhausted she could barely stand, and when a woman belonging to another party rose from her place, Paul swiftly guided Cameron to the seat with a proprietary air of consideration.

Cameron thrilled to his touch on her elbow, and she constantly cautioned herself that his behavior was for the baby more than for her. Even as she sat, he stood close by, reminding her of a guard dog. Though she liked dogs and though his attentiveness touched her, she feared the strength of her own reactions. She *didn't* want to be in love with Paul. He was being attentive to her, but it was because of the baby.

Cameron had always thought of herself as modern, a feminist. But a tiny, stupid part of her wished that what Mary Anne had predicted would come true, that Paul would ask to marry her. Why on Earth would a sane, mature woman wish such a thing? It wasn't as though he was in love with her! It would be marriage for the sake of the baby, which wasn't something she was sure she believed in.

She crossed her legs in her corduroy bell-bottoms; none of her pants had yet become snug. She wondered how soon they would. Over her corduroys, she wore a long, lacy top in dark brown, close around her breasts but extending loose below, a top she thought she would be able to wear as a maternity top. Mary Anne had helped her choose a necklace in jet and smoky quartz, which had been a gift from Mary Anne herself, along with the matching earrings, and she had persuaded Cameron to wear her long hair down, unbraided, which always made Cameron feel frivolous—entirely unprepared to, say, ride her bicycle or run five miles. Indeed, her hair had gotten caught on something on the passenger door of Paul's vehicle, and he'd had to reach over the gear shift to untangle the tresses.

Which had been yet another opportunity to notice that though Paul's feelings toward her hadn't changed, hers toward him had done so.

She studied him for a moment as he stood over her. He wore a loosely knotted, narrow necktie with his olive-colored shirt, as neckties were required at Rick's. His pants were dark brown twill.

How had she managed the charade they had practiced for so many years—four, at least—of simply *pretending* to be his girlfriend? Had she kept up the pretense because she *was* attracted to him and wanted to prevent him finding a girlfriend, a real girlfriend, other than her?

She had seen him many times before shirtless or in swim trunks, even on midnight skinny-dipping expeditions, but she had been so convinced of his lack of worth as a partner that she had ignored his physical attractions. Well, it had seemed that way at the time. Now, she tried to think him out of consideration as a partner, but it wasn't working as well as in the past. In her mind, suddenly, he was the *only* partner for her. But what kind of fool adopted these ideas about a man sworn against matrimony?

Should she aim for something different? Simply try for boyfriend-girlfriend lovers?

Good grief, he was even opposed to that—or had always said so.

On the other hand, she could settle for Sean Devlin.

No. She remembered what Paul had suggested, that perhaps Sean told Cameron too much of himself and his feelings, too much for her to find him attractive. It was true she felt that she *knew* Sean. She also knew Paul, but there was so much of Paul she didn't know. Paul would always interest her because they were different from each other.

But did she interest Paul in the same way?

It didn't seem so.

During the ride to the restaurant, Cameron had longed to blurt out, "To what do I owe this honor?" But what if there *was* no special occasion, as her intuition told her was the case?

Fortunately, thanks to an increase in vitamin B6 and frequent protein-rich snacks, she felt less nauseated than she had for a week and was looking forward to hearing the specials.

"Are you all right?"

Her thoughts must have shown. "Fine. Fine."

The maître d' came to seat them at last, at a table for two near one of the windows upstairs, now dark, but also near the fireplace.

When they sat down, she told him, "Your plot has failed. I'm hungry."

He glanced up from the menu and grinned, his face creasing attractively, his dark eyes on her. Cameron remembered making love with him, recalled that even then she had felt a certain aloofness and reserve, as though there were an invisible barrier between them, which she recognized as his not wanting to commit. Not even to commit himself to being a little in love with her during the moments they were intimate.

Cameron thought again of the fact that it was after she'd said she had no idea what part he wanted in their baby's life that he'd asked her to join him for dinner. Well, seeing that she had no silly romantic hopes for this occasion—really she didn't—she may as well try to get some answers.

"The baby," she said.

He blinked at her, as though unsure which baby she meant. She half expected him to start glancing around the restaurant in the hope of seeing the one of whom she spoke.

"For heaven's sake," she hissed. "The baby. I want to know what part you plan to play in the baby's life."

He stared at her for a moment, then grabbed his water glass. "I—I'm going to be the baby's father."

Cameron thought he looked as though he might choke,

and she didn't know whether she felt more sorry for him, herself or their child. She recalled Sean's text message haiku, promising to care for her and the baby. She said sternly, "You *are* the baby's father. I just want to know how you're going to integrate the fact. What you're going to do."

Paul was keenly aware that the hero of any of those stupid books Cameron read would never have made love to her in the first place without being married to her; her ideal romantic world was that represented in books written for nice women in the 1940s and 1950s. Now that he had slept with her and she was pregnant, he felt constantly called upon to act without chivalry in order to be true to himself. The correct thing to do, according to many people, probably including his own father and possibly his mother, would be to ask Cameron to marry him. Briefly, he considered asking her to marry him in the hope that she would refuse.

But he didn't think she *would* refuse.

Darting away from the picture of marriage with Cameron, a picture with too much finality for the moment, he said, "I intend to have regular visits with our child. Weekends, probably. You and I will work it out."

To his horror, Cameron's eyes filled with tears.

She said, "Sorry. It's morning sickness. I'll be back." And she stood up hurriedly from the table, so keen to hide her face from everyone in the restaurant but especially Paul that she slammed right into David Cureux, who was escorting his daughter.

"Excuse me," she said and made herself smile. "Morning sickness."

Oh, God. The pain was excruciating, and yet all Paul had said was what she'd expected. He was immature, was against marriage for reasons which made no sense to anyone, and that only meant—how well she knew it— that he'd not yet met the woman he wanted to marry.

She did not have morning sickness, but she went to the ladies' room anyhow, determined to keep up the pretense. She just had to get herself together, to accept that this was no fairy tale, no happily-ever-after story. In any case, the happy ending she wanted was a healthy baby—this baby. She didn't want a man who was apathetic about her to offer to marry her just for the baby. Who would want to marry under those circumstances? Well, some women would, but she wasn't one of them.

In the restroom, she stood in front of the mirror in thankful solitude and repeated a series of affirmations she had written for herself in the determination to take her through a safe, healthy, pregnancy, labor and birth. "I am a natural mother. My hips were made to push babies into the world. My body was made to carry babies…."

"NICE GOING," Bridget said as she and her father stood over Paul's and Cameron's table. They had been guided to a table across the small room by the mâitre d' but had both left it to speak to Paul, who had stood up when Cameron rose to leave the table. "Being your charming self, I can see."

"It's…morning sickness," Paul said uneasily, gazing in the direction Cameron had gone. Despite his words, he'd been sure that Cameron was starting to cry, not that she was ill. What on Earth had he said to make her cry?

He felt rather than saw his father's eyes on him in disappointment and disgust. Paul said, "I think I'll check on her. If you see the waiter, tell him we'll be right back." Unless Cameron really was sick.

But she wasn't.

"You're going to make her sit through dinner with morning sickness?" Bridget demanded.

Irritated, he skirted the table so as not to have to shove his sister out of the way.

Bridget watched him go. Calmly, she removed a small vial from her purse, opened the lid and emptied the contents into Paul's water glass. She capped the bottle, dropped it back into her purse and looked defiantly at her father.

David Cureux shook his head, and Bridget watched him decide to spend his breath. "Errant nonsense," he told her, taking her elbow to steer her back to their table.

Bridget knew her father completely denied that love potions possessed any efficacy whatsoever. He believed they did not work. But just now, she thought with affectionate pity, he sounded rather as though he wished they did.

PAUL WAS WAITING in the hallway when Cameron stepped out of the ladies' room.

"What are you doing here?" she asked.

"Are you all right?"

"I'm fine."

"Will you be able to eat?"

Was he hoping that she wouldn't be able, so that they

would have to leave? "Certainly," she answered. "There's nothing to worry about. It's all part of pregnancy." All part of *this* pregnancy, she thought.

He nodded silently and gestured for her to proceed him down the short hallway and back upstairs. When they reached the room where they'd been seated, Cameron made a point of smiling broadly as she waved to Bridget and David.

She sat down at the table with Paul, and the waiter appeared in the doorway and gave them a questioning look.

Cameron opened the menu. "I'm ready."

Paul nodded to the waiter, who came to the table and recited the specials. Cameron picked the salmon, Paul duckling in apricot sauce. The waiter offered them wine, and Paul shook his head, reaching determinedly for his water again.

Cameron, who had drained her own glass, asked for more, and Paul offered her his glass but she said, "I'm fine for the moment."

Paul gazed across the table at her, sorry that he'd made her cry. Whatever he'd done, he'd obviously been a jerk. Drinking his water, he thought how beautiful she looked. He loved her small face, her smile, her long hair that reminded him of a girl in a fairy tale. He was proud that she was having his child, and yet he thought that pride bestial, chauvinistic, all wrong.

Yet shouldn't he ask her to marry him? She would say yes, and, well, they'd work it out. They did get along, didn't fight like cats and dogs, and were attracted to each other. Well, he was to her. And she'd seemed so to him that night...the night they'd conceived the baby.

It occurred to him that if he proposed she might say no, aware that he didn't really want to marry her. Which he didn't, did he? It was ridiculous to think of being married, of having this baby together. *I'm not ready for this.*

He took another drink of water, then drew in his breath and said, "I think we should move in together."

Her face flooded, and she recalled how recently he had made her cry, and now he also guessed *why,* what the reason must be. It was because he'd said plainly that he wanted to be a part-time dad. "Why?" she asked coldly. "You don't want to be a full-time dad."

Paul tried to speak and felt as though his tongue had been immobilized. Could he say that he *did* want to be a full-time dad—or even a full-time partner?

"Don't worry," she said, a bit sharply. "You're safe. No, Paul, I don't think we should move in together. I can't see anything good coming of it." As he stared at her, expressionless, as though she'd slapped him, she recalled that he was taking her out to this very nice dinner and had cooked for her recently. Well, so what?

Paul closed his eyes, then picked up his water glass and drained it. Why did he feel so miserable? He should be jumping up and down for joy. He didn't have to live with her. They would raise their child from different houses.

A depressing picture. The picture of he and Cameron living together in one house, raising their child, was so much *happier.* He said, "I want to live with you—and the baby."

"I doubt it," she answered. "Let's not talk about it anymore." Cameron felt her appetite ebbing and was glad to see the waiter approach with the soup.

BY THE TIME Paul turned his truck into her driveway that night, he'd decided that kissing her good-night might earn him a slap in the face. But he really needed more information. Parking in front of her house, he touched her arm before she could reach for the door. "Wait."

Cameron looked at him. The look was dispassionate, but he knew the vulnerability beneath.

"What if I had asked you to marry me?"

She said, "You didn't," and reached for the door handle.

"Cameron." He touched her hair, couldn't help it.

She spun round. "You're suddenly attracted to me because I'm carrying your child. It's entirely biological and means *nothing.*"

He shook his head.

"What?" she asked.

"It's not—just—attraction." How could he explain? "It's something else. I want to take care of you."

He thought he saw her soften, and he put his hand on the side of her small face and leaned toward her.

She let him kiss her, and he slid his hand down, pulled her closer.

She drew back, shaking her head.

At least she hadn't hit him. "What?"

"I don't want to play with this," she said.

He tried making sense of her words. "Who's playing?"

"I think you are."

"That's not fair. I just asked you for a commitment about an hour ago."

She squinted at him. "Was that what you were doing?"

"Yes!"

She nodded slowly and reached for the door handle again. "Thanks for dinner."

Paul wracked his brain for means to convince her of his seriousness. Nothing occurred to him. He said again, "Would it have been different?"

She froze. "If you'd asked me to marry you? How the hell should I know?" She looked into his eyes. "Because in order to ask that question, you'd have had to be a different person."

That was a slap all right.

"Good night," she said.

He just nodded and watched in the headlights as she walked toward the house, watched the two dog shapes rise from the porch, watched her unlock the door and go inside, waited until the lights went on inside.

Did she mean she wanted him to be a different person?

Maybe, Paul. Maybe she wants you to be the kind of person who believes two people can get married and stay married and remain faithful and kind to one another all their lives.

If he wasn't that kind of person... Well, he wasn't.

But something niggled at him, the question no one had answered. He looked at the clock on the dash and saw it was only nine. He headed for his mother's.

Myrtle Hollow

CLARE SANK DOWN at the kitchen table, recalling a recent conversation with her ex-husband. Now, here was Paul, asking the very questions she didn't want to answer. Well, no, that wasn't true. He didn't know the questions to ask.

"They were travelers. They lived in a VW bus all painted with flowers, and it had broken down halfway up this hollow. The man came to the door in the middle of the night and told me so, said his wife was in labor and they'd been looking for me, knew I was a midwife. At first, I said they should call an ambulance. He said his wife was terrified of hospitals and having a really bad time, and couldn't I just look at her?

"I said I would and that I would take her to the hospital if she needed to go."

Across the table, Paul watched his mother's face harden.

"I got there, her water had broken and was meconium-stained and there were no fetal heart tones. I examined her to see if I could get the baby out—thinking perhaps I could get him breathing. And it was a case of true cephalopelvic disproportion or CPD—in fact, only one of two cases I've seen my whole career. The other was initially my client, and I referred her to a physician because the child had to be born by cesarean.

"In this case, she was not my client, and they had waited too long to seek help. I think they must have had no prenatal guidance. I drove them to the hospital, and she had a cesarean."

She stopped speaking abruptly.

Paul said, "I'm afraid of Cameron having that. Not a cesarean. That CPD."

"If it happens, which is extremely rare, we'll know about it with plenty of warning, and she will have a physician." Clare rose from the table. "And now it's time for me to head off to bed."

Paul didn't move. "Didn't that stillbirth happen right before Dad moved out?"

"Yes," she answered. "Around that time."

"Were there problems with the hospital? Did they blame you?"

"I was exonerated," she said. "Fairly soon."

Paul was surprised to hear it. Although his father had been an obstetrician, there wasn't much love lost between other local obstetricians and his mother. The medical people thought all homebirths were dangerous. His mother thought most hospital births were. She also knew, as did Paul, that a huge number of unnecessary complications and cesarean sections occurred because of unnecessary technical intervention in hospitals.

He rose from the table at last and said, "Well, 'night, Mom," and kissed her cheek.

She hugged him briefly and said, "Watch out for deer on your way home."

Clare closed the door after him and waited till she saw his headlights turn out of her yard before she began switching off the lights in the cabin. There was no reason for him to know the rest, to know *how* she'd come to be exonerated. She'd been blameless in the fetal death, and that had been the conclusion reached in the end. She'd done what she'd had to in order to make sure that happened.

A quiet rage still bubbled inside her at the memory of being falsely accused, of her feelings of helplessness and impotence when faced with those accusations. At first, she'd been angry at the couple, for what they'd done, for two things they'd done. But those poor sorrowing people. Even then, her anger toward them hadn't lasted long.

She thought about Paul. His question had arisen from fear for Cameron—and the baby. Whether he acknowledged it or not, he did love Cameron.

I need to tell him everything, she thought. Abruptly, she felt shame that she hadn't told him tonight, had protected herself instead. She'd always tried to be the best mother she could be to him, but she felt that tonight she had really lied to him, lied by omission. What she had to relate made her feel dirty and degraded, but now, concealing it from the son who was so dissatisfied with the spoken reasons for his parents' divorce, she felt even worse.

She could call him on the phone now. And he would drive back.

She looked at the clock.

No. She would find time tomorrow—find a place in his day.

CHAPTER EIGHT

"IT'S GOING TO BE very simple. You will be maid of honor, and *probably* Graham's dissertation advisor will be best man. They've remained good friends, and Graham wants him but he's not absolutely sure the man will be free that weekend."

"You want a *pregnant* maid of honor?" Cameron said. They were in a Charleston bridal shop looking at dresses, something Mary Anne was determined to do before her mother could get involved in the process. "I'll have to wear a maternity dress."

Mary Anne frowned. "You won't be that big. We're having the wedding on Valentine's Day."

"I will be obviously pregnant."

"Well, I don't mind, so you shouldn't. I'm honored to have my little first cousin once removed in the ceremony."

"Considering the baby has Paul's genes," Cameron remarked philosophically, "it might be good for the little one to be introduced to the idea of weddings and marriage early in life."

They'd asked the saleswoman to let them look at

dresses on racks and the dresses in the store's books before receiving further help. This allowed them a degree of privacy.

"Tell me again what he said last night," Mary Anne urged.

"He said he thought we should move in together." She hadn't mentioned the kiss in the car to her cousin, thinking it unseemly to do so. "Romantic, no?"

Mary Anne read the sarcasm. "Maybe he's working himself up to a more permanent proposal. Maybe he wants to give the whole thing a test ride."

"He's *had* that," Cameron replied bitterly.

Mary Anne rolled her eyes. "I meant nothing so crude."

"He's known me for half his life—at least. And he knows me *well,* and I know him well." Her cell phone rang and she took it from her purse.

Paul.

She considered not answering.

Instead, she waved to Mary Anne and headed for the exit as she answered.

"Hi."

"Hi. Where are you?"

"In Charleston. Where are you?"

"Outside your house. It's my lunch hour." Paul worked weekends—such was the life of a zookeeper. "Where's your spare key? You moved it."

She frowned. "Inside the dog house." The dog house that no dog used.

"That's creative."

"Why are you going in my house?"

"Mmm…a bird is stuck in there."

"You're kidding." She said, "I saw a mouse the other day. It's that time of year. I hate them. I should get a cat. What's a bird doing in there?"

"No idea. I've seen it try to fly out the window. It's going to kill itself if… Ah. There. Bye, little bird. When are you coming home?"

"When we feel like it. Mary Anne's looking for a wedding dress, and we're going out for dinner."

"Two nights in a row. That morning sickness *must* be better."

Cameron remembered the horrible moment the night before when she'd burst into tears at the table. "Yes. I have to go."

"Want to go to the movies tomorrow?"

"Okay."

She returned to the bridal store and repeated the conversation to Mary Anne.

"At least he's asking you out!" Mary Anne exclaimed. "You want him to, don't you?"

"I think so."

Cameron sat with Mary Anne. She, the store model and Mary Anne took turns trying on wedding gowns, a ritual that made Cameron depressed. She'd never thought of herself as particularly traditional or determined to be married one day. In fact, she was accepting of the fact she might never be married. And if she did get married, she couldn't see herself doing the whole white-dress-with-a-train thing.

But expecting a baby changed everything, and now her unmarried condition rankled. Paul's behavior struck her as ungentlemanly in the extreme, yet Paul was a man who always opened doors for women, who *knew* how to behave immaculately.

So what's wrong with me?

She tried to be cheerful, to tell Mary Anne how beautiful she was, and to remind herself how *happy* she actually was to be pregnant, despite the complications, including her fear. She was in love with the baby. Paul really didn't matter.

THE FLOWERS were on the kitchen table, nothing so predictable as a dozen red roses but a huge fall bouquet with a wild, woodsy look.

A note in Paul's hand lay on the kitchen table. *A little bird brought these.*

Cameron swallowed. There had been no bird in her house. He'd been bringing her flowers.

She searched the bouquet and found an envelope. She opened it to find a card with a horn of plenty on it. He'd written, *Thank you for having dinner with me. Paul.*

At least he sent flowers, she told herself, trying not to be disappointed in the message, which hardly seemed one of love. Less affectionate, in fact, than Sean's ordinary text messages. Of course, if Paul were someone she'd just met, she'd have been charmed by the message—by the entire gesture.

For a moment, the terror came, terror of miscarriage, of losing the baby, a terror which far eclipsed any fear of the pain of labor.

She forced herself to walk in the bedroom, look in the mirror and voice her affirmations. But it was hard to summon the emotion she needed to believe that everything would be all right.

CLARE FOUND IT HARD to find a time to tell Paul the rest of the story about the stillbirth. Every time she was near him, so was the rest of the family. Cameron's second prenatal visit—as well as Christmas—was nearly upon them when Paul finally showed up alone one day, his errand being to pick up her trash and recycling and take them to the transfer station.

Clare insisted on carrying a bag of aluminum cans— accumulated over months—to his truck. She'd vowed to say it. She did not look at him. "You've asked many times why your father walked out. Well, it was because of that stillbirth."

Paul stared in disbelief.

"No, not because of the stillbirth, but because of things that happened afterward." Clare could not remember feeling so much shame in the years since those horrible days. "The hospital accused me of negligence and was determined to see me stop practicing. I had clients with babies due soon, or I might have chosen to fight it the proper way, in court.

"But you see, the witnesses were gone. They got in their hippie van and drove off before they were properly questioned." Clare could not look at her son and so had no idea how he was taking this. "The chief of obstetrics offered to make it all 'go away.' Those were his words.

'I can make this all go away, Clare.'" She took a breath. "If I would sleep with him."

Paul, listening, was horrified. Less horrified by the behavior of the chief of obstetrics than by his mother's response, which he could already guess.

"I did it to allow me to keep following my vocation. Your father learned of it, and it was all over."

Paul suddenly felt equally infuriated with his father, who had overreacted. Surely counseling or…forgiveness? And yet it must have been almost impossible. Paul himself found he didn't want to forgive his mother. Part of him had wanted to know, yet now he wished he didn't know. He felt a surge of hatred for all of them—his weak mother, his unforgiving father, the corrupt chief of obstetrics, the idiot parents of the stillborn child. In fact, his mind, heart and soul overflowed with conflicting emotions.

I wish I didn't know.

He'd spent most of his life feeling bitter toward his parents for being divorced for no reason.

Now he'd been given a "reason," and it was terrible. This sordid drama had been going on while he and Bridget were small children. But even then, they had *felt* it.

He heard the anger in his voice when he said, "Is there any reason at all to think that Cameron might have—what you said—CPD?"

"CPD means that the baby's head is too big to pass through the mother's pelvis. We will know more as her labor approaches, but I think she can have a vaginal birth. We'll see what Dr. Henderson says. In any case, the scenario will not be like the one twenty-five years ago. I'll remind you that the woman involved was *not* my client."

Paul heard the steely sound in his mother's voice and heard the anger, and her anger was more like fury.

"Then why didn't you fight it?"

"Because it would have taken me into the courts, and there would have been long delays, and I would have been barred from attending homebirths. I could not fight it and continue to take care of the women who were depending on me."

"And you weren't licensed, and you're still not licensed."

"You know why. I'm not going to discuss it in this context."

Paul did know why, just as he could feel his mother shaking with rage, looking as if she would spit nails. West Virginia had a long tradition of midwifery. Practicing midwifery "without a license" was deemed illegal, and then room was made for certified nurse-midwives to practice. At the time that law was passed, his mother already had ten years' experience with homebirth; she had chosen not to leave her family to go to school and become an RN and then a certified nurse-midwife.

"It's a misdemeanor," he whispered.

"Yes, until something like *that* disaster happens. I didn't want it in the courts, Paul. For a host of reasons."

"So you traded yourself."

He'd gone too far. He saw it.

"You don't know anything about it! You think this is

something I'm proud of? Why do you think we kept it from you?" She was almost shouting.

He almost shouted back, "Why didn't you keep on keeping it from me?"

"Because your sister knows, and I thought you were old enough to hear it, too."

"Bridget knows?"

"Yes, I told her a few years ago." Clare would not reveal the circumstances under which she'd told her daughter this shameful secret from her own past. It wasn't Paul's business but Bridget's. During the birth of her first child, Bridget's labor had abruptly stopped. With only her mother in the room, Bridget had revealed an instance of sexual violation from her college years. Clare remembered the time well, remembered her certainty that Bridget was in trouble. But Bridget, when she'd answered the phone, had denied everything.

And left Clare more certain than ever.

So Clare had told Bridget what had happened to her, her anger joining with her daughter's.

And labor had progressed again.

So often that was the case. And though the incident in Clare's past was horrible to her, she had come to see the gift in the horror. That she could relate, just a little bit, to women who had been violated and abused. And so she had become a better midwife.

Paul remembered what he was supposed to be doing, collecting garbage and recyclables. He walked back to the porch to grab the last trash bag. His mother stood near the tailgate, arms wrapped around herself in a posture that reminded him of Cameron—but only Cameron recently.

Clare dropped her arms. "Well, that's the story, and now you know it."

"Why did you tell me now?" he asked again.

"Because you asked about the birth."

"You told me about the birth."

Clare knew what he was asking. "I thought it would be good for you to know."

"Like castor oil?"

"I never gave you castor oil in your life."

"This is about Cameron, isn't it? You and Dad decided this, didn't you? To tell me. You're trying to get me to marry Cameron." Paul heard how childish he sounded. But part of him was the small boy seeing his father leave, saying, *But you're our dad! You can't leave!*

"I would never try to get you to do something you don't want to do. Not in your adult life and nothing so important as marriage."

"Then it's Dad."

"Paul, you've made this bed, and you better lie in it. And that means if people think the less of you for getting a woman pregnant and not marrying her, that's something you're going to have to deal with. It has nothing to do with me, and you can't stop people feeling what they will."

Her voice had stopped shaking. Paul felt no censure from his mother on the subject of Cameron, and that was a relief. His mother truly had no opinion on the subject. But his father… At the restaurant, Paul had felt his father's disapproval in waves across the room.

Well, his mother was right. He was an adult.

He wished he didn't feel so much like a child.

He wasn't ready to confront his father, but he wanted to talk to someone about what his mother had said.

There was only one person he wanted to talk to.

AN OLD MAZDA with a crushed passenger door was parked diagonally across a spot for the handicapped in the parking lot of the Women's Resource Center. Another car, a new Volvo Paul recognized as belonging to Sean Devlin, was parked in another space. As Paul swung open the glass front door, he immediately saw the person who must have driven the Mazda.

Over six feet tall, wearing work clothes and a dark slouch hat with a feather in the band, smelling of sweat, cigarette smoke and alcohol, the man said, "You tell me where the bitch has gone!"

Cameron, five foot five in her running shoes and looking smaller than ever, wearing new pants because her others had become too tight, stared impassively at the angry intruder, Sean towering over her. "No," she said. "And you need to leave this building, or I'm calling the police to have you removed."

He turned his unimaginative and profane vocabulary on Cameron, who turned away to go into her office and phone the police.

"Don't you turn away when I'm talking to you!" He grabbed her shoulders roughly and spun her around.

"Hey," said Sean, stepping toward the villain.

The creep did not release Cameron, and Paul threw an

arm upward between them, lifting the hands from
Cameron's shoulders.

A fist like a sledgehammer connected with the side
of his head.

Paul slammed his fist into the man's stomach and
drove his knee into his groin.

The guy took one breath, seemed to crumple, but then
staggered forward, grabbed Paul's head and sunk his
teeth into Paul's ear, and Sean threw a punch, which hit
Paul instead of its target.

"Oh, God, sorry!" Sean cried.

Enough was enough.

Paul twisted the chief assailant's arm backward and
used his leg as leverage to flip the bigger man onto his back.

His opponent grabbed Paul's knees, not giving up. As
Paul went down, taking the opportunity to slam the heel
of his hand into the guy's nose, Cameron was there,
saying, "The police are coming, Jerry! Stay where you
are and make it easy for all of us."

But Jerry, as though deaf, was still determined to get
in his retaliation against Paul, now pulling his hair and
preparing to gouge out his eyes.

Cameron, who had the same martial arts training as
Paul, slammed a sidekick into Jerry's knee. The sound
was sickening, and as Jerry released Paul, Cameron fled
to the ladies' room.

Paul distanced himself from Jerry and, exchanging
glances with an abashed-looking Sean, got on his own
phone to tell the police to send an ambulance, as well.
Cameron had done damage.

Certain that Jerry, who was cursing volubly, couldn't go anywhere—and not caring if he did, as long as it was somewhere else—Paul followed Cameron into the bathroom where she had finished vomiting and was rinsing her face.

"I hurt him, didn't I?" she whispered. "I didn't mean to."

"I wish you'd stayed out of it."

"He was hurting you! Oh, God, I'm going to throw up again." She retreated to a cubicle, where he heard her retching.

Paul noticed blood dripping on the ground. It was from his ear, which he started washing, hoping the guy didn't have anything that would kill him.

"This isn't a safe place for you to work."

She emerged from the cubicle. "It usually is. He wanted to know where the safe house for battered women is."

"Lovely. And you're all that was standing between him and that information."

"Sean was here."

"That's the scary part. Your Jerry's the kind of guy who is undeterred by your six-foot-three hero. How many creeps like him are out there, wanting to know the same thing? You need a security guard in here, Cameron."

"It has been said before."

"Do something about it."

"Funding?"

"I don't want you working here. You could have lost the baby."

"I didn't think it was *me* you were worried about," she murmured.

"It *is* you. If you miscarried, you could have bled to death!"

Cameron swallowed, mollified. They heard sirens, and she opened the restroom door. Jerry had managed to drag himself up and was now standing on one leg, leaning on the door. He pushed open the door, and neither they, nor Sean, who sat moodily on a chair in the waiting room, tried to stop him.

Sean said, "I'm sorry, Paul. I have no experience with fights. I should have left you to it. Or done something helpful. Are you all right?"

"You didn't hurt me." Paul put slight emphasis on the first word, hoping to convey that Sean's feeble punch couldn't have hurt an eight-year-old.

"What about you?" Sean asked Cameron, standing up and gazing down at her.

Paul saw the other man's expression, the sort of forlorn concern, and thought, *Shit.*

Sean was in love with Cameron.

Of course, she didn't love him back. He wasn't her type. Paul considered the question of what Cameron's type might be and answered the question easily, brushing aside her juvenile infatuation with Graham Corbett—who was somewhat Sean's type. What was Cameron's type?

Me.

He gave Sean a smile dripping with pity as the door opened and the first cop came in.

TWO HOURS LATER, Cameron sat at her kitchen table while Paul roasted red bell peppers over the flames on the gas range, minding a pot of rice on another burner and a skillet in which he was sautéing tofu.

Statements taken, police gone with Jerry, Paul had thrown Cameron's mountain bike in the back of his truck and wished Sean Devlin a pleasant evening. On the way home, he'd told her the reason for his visit to the resource center, to repeat what his mother had told him. Then, before giving her time to react, he'd told her again that she needed to get a security guard in "that place" or quit.

Cameron had said she would investigate the security guard plan and call an emergency meeting of the board.

Paul had then begun analyzing his own actions in the fight, saying he should have struck more aggressively earlier.

"He was unusually…tenacious," Cameron had said, trying to think what Paul could have done differently, and the ideas were all severe. Put his foot on the guy's throat.

Now she said, "Your poor mother."

"Why poor her?"

Cameron found the question incredible. "It was almost like rape. Can you imagine? She had to have sex with that creep to preserve her vocation and be able to help those women."

"She shouldn't have done it," he answered firmly.

"She felt that she had to."

"Well, she didn't have to. I can see why my dad was angry. Except he shouldn't have left."

"Oh, please. Of course, you can see why he was angry. And look, I feel for you and all, but even if it wasn't something your mother should have done, imagine her feelings now, imagine having to live with that—and feeling that she had to tell you."

"But why did she have to tell me?"

Cameron rolled her eyes. "Probably both your parents are mystified that, although successful marriages *do* happen and you have been witness to the fact, you feel a total lack of faith in matrimony. Probably they're hoping you'll marry me."

"My mother said she's not."

"Thank you, Clare."

"No—I mean, she's not attached to it. She likes you. She doesn't want me *not* to marry you. She just wants me to make up my own mind."

"Then, I'm in agreement with her. Adding that *my* mind also has to get made up."

Paul didn't turn around. Suddenly he found himself considering again the similarity between Graham Corbett and Sean Devlin. And there was no doubt Devlin was a good-looking guy. He frowned. "You didn't even like me kissing you the other night."

"Because I felt as though you felt that you *had* to do it. I hate things that are forced. And 'I think we should move in together' isn't going to win any Most Romantic Phrases contest."

Paul spun around. "I was sincere."

"I'm not going to give you lessons in courtship. Thank you for making dinner, by the way."

Paul smiled. "At least I got one thing right."

"What's that?"

He put cheese and crackers on the table in front of her

and helped himself to some. "You understand that I'm courting you."

A small place inside her, like a spring bud that has survived a frost, began to open slightly. Her heart felt warm, her cheeks got bright, as well.

Paul turned his attention to the stove, stirring the tofu, turning the bell peppers. "Hey, we're preparing a winter solstice festival at the zoo. Tell me you want to volunteer."

"To do what?" Cameron asked suspiciously.

"Face-painting?" Paul turned. "We'll have a Yule log and a parade through the zoo and a cardboard sled derby down the sledding hill near the entrance."

"I hope you're having everyone sign waivers."

"Of course I am. When have I ever been incautious?" Paul demanded.

"I'll help," Cameron agreed, asking herself how much supervision of *parents* would be her lot. So many times when parents brought kids to activities at the zoo, they behaved as though they'd hired a babysitter.

Paul said, "Thanks," and put a cup of red raspberry leaf tea in front of her. Having learned it was good for pregnancy, Cameron had drunk nothing else for days but raspberry leaf tea and water.

"Cameron, after hearing the story of that stillbirth, are you sure you still want to have a homebirth?"

"If it's safe. So far, it seems as though it will be. But the end of July is a long way off. In any case, that woman wasn't your mother's client, so your mom didn't know if her pelvis was big enough or not. Your mother wouldn't have let that woman attempt a homebirth. She's not a cretin."

Paul accepted what Cameron said. He didn't believe his mother's becoming a CNM would make her a better midwife in any way. And fortunately, Dr. Henderson was willing to see her clients. He would tell Clare if he saw anything abnormal. And if hospital transport became necessary, at least he would have met the pregnant woman.

In any case, he and Cameron were due to go to a prenatal appointment with the physician this week.

A few minutes later, Paul sat across from her at the kitchen table. He had thought about her all day every day ever since the night they'd had dinner together, if not before. The feeling had been growing in him since the first night they'd made love.

"It's ridiculous," he said, "if my mother told me because she thought it would make a difference in how I conduct *my* life."

Cameron had nothing to say to this. Just stabbed another piece of tofu and scooped up some rice.

"I mean, they told me they got divorced because they stopped getting along, and I can grasp that what happened was certainly an impediment to getting along. But it's not like *I'm* fated to get divorced because they did."

It was the first time Cameron had heard him say this. She asked, "Do you have a fever?"

"Ha ha. Want to play Scrabble after dinner?"

"Sure."

Their Scrabble games were a long tradition. They played open dictionary so as to improve their knowledge. During Cameron's turns, Paul played his guitar for her, during his turns, she did yoga or practiced tae kwon do.

"I might get too tired," she warned.

"I expect such histrionics whenever you're losing."

"I never lose."

It was one of the nicest evenings Cameron had ever spent with Paul. She loved listening to him play his guitar and sing. He played many of her favorite folk songs and her favorite of his original numbers. While he was taking his turns, she washed the dishes. But when there were still at least fifteen tiles left—and Paul, unfortunately, ahead—Cameron admitted, "I can barely keep my eyes open."

"A likely story." But he smiled as he put down his guitar. "Why don't I tuck you in?"

Cameron wanted it and yet was afraid. She knew how strong biology was, knew that he could be—and probably was—attracted to her simply because she was carrying his child. But how silly she was being. She'd been foolish to reject his suggestion that they move in together. The formality of marriage meant little to her; the commitment was what mattered.

But the commitment wasn't there. Well, Paul's only possible commitment was to their baby—at present a two-month-old fetus.

But she was attracted to him. No, she loved him. Loved him as her best friend. Was practically in love with him. Was in love with him. "Okay," she said.

Why are you doing this, Cameron? You've read He's Just Not That Into You. Cameron considered that book the bible on disinterested men. And Paul's behavior appeared in more than one chapter.

They went into her bedroom. Cameron routinely slept naked. She had brushed her teeth after dinner. Without looking at Paul, she peeled off her jeans, T-shirt and underwear, releasing her breasts from her bra. She pulled back the covers and got into bed.

Paul sat down beside her. He touched her hair and the side of her face, his whole body alive with wanting her.

Cameron saw what she did to him and reminded herself that it was not the equivalent of love.

He bent over her and kissed her, and Cameron let herself kiss him back.

He said, "I love you, Cameron."

Cameron's heart felt as though it would break free from her chest. He had never said that to her before—not in a way that meant that he loved her romantically. But that was, she knew, what he meant now.

She said nothing, just let her lips meet his again, feeling the touch of his tongue.

He drew down the covers to look at her and pulled off his own T-shirt and jeans.

Cameron's lips touched his back as he undressed, moved around his waist and down his body.

"Oh, girl," he whispered, gently touching her hair, following a tress down past her waist. "Rapunzel."

Cameron tried to let go of her fear. She hadn't been afraid the night their child was conceived because she hadn't been in love with him and hadn't had the sense to fear falling in love with him.

He had a way of lying on top of her that moved her heart, because he seemed anxious that his weight not crush her, as though she were a fragile thing he feared to injure.

His mouth caressed her nipple, and she shuddered, telling herself to let go and trust him. *It will kill me if he leaves.*

He was doing nothing to her that other men had not done before. But it was Paul and she loved him. She barely knew him as a lover. There was that Halloween night in college and the night their child was conceived—and that was it.

They did not speak—or little. Cameron wished he would, that he would tell her his innermost thoughts. And yet she was fascinated with him in part because she did not know those thoughts. She felt as though, even were he to say what he was thinking, it would be an incomplete story, with more chapters always to unfold.

And now, she let go and was not afraid, because she had no choice, because the way he touched her she couldn't bear to turn herself off. She let him open her legs, let him touch her.

She let soft cries escape her, seeming to remember some innocence in her long before.

Later, much later, he asked, "Can I stay?"

Surprised, she said, "Of course."

"You were opposed to our moving in together."

"You've only asked to spend the night. Not to spend months or years." If only his moving in together had held the proviso of his never leaving.

Instead, she had the feeling that Paul simply wanted to play house.

He hugged her, her back nestled to his front. "You might be grateful for another pair of hands when the baby comes."

"I will be," she said. "As long as I don't end up with a second child to take care of."

He stiffened. "I don't deserve that."

Cameron instantly regretted her words. "I'm sorry."

"There are people in this world," he remarked conversationally, "who see not rushing into marriage as a sign of maturity."

"Who said anything about marriage?" she asked.

He made a sound that seemed to call her question insincere.

Abruptly annoyed, she gathered the sheet to her chest, sat up, and turned toward him. "You know, I do want you to leave."

"What did I do?"

"Forget it," Cameron said. "You are who you are. No one should have to explain these things to you. *I'm pregnant, Paul.* And you claim to love me. But you can't bring yourself to do anything more than moving in together. Then I let you know that maybe *I* don't want to marry someone who obviously doesn't want to marry me, and *you* make these sounds like I'm madly in love with you."

"Okay," he said. "Will you marry me?"

"Get out!" she cried, looking for something to throw. Mariah, who had been lying on the floor, growled low in her throat.

He slipped away from Cameron and grabbed his

clothes. "You're behaving irrationally," he said. "I just asked you to marry me because you want me to want to marry you, and now you're throwing me out."

"That's not why you ask someone to marry you," she answered, lying down on her bed, listening to him dress. She wanted him to come near her, to kiss her, before he left, but he didn't.

CHAPTER NINE

THE MALE SAKI had diarrhea and was dangerously dehydrated. He had to be caught, and Paul needed to be on hand to help the vet. And this was the day he was supposed to go to Dr. Henderson's with Cameron. Well, she was going to have to go alone.

He called her and told her what was happening and that he couldn't make it.

"Fine," she said and hung up.

He hadn't had an actual conversation with her since he'd left her house the night they'd made love and she'd told him to leave.

Words she'd said—that she was pregnant and that he couldn't bring himself to ask her to marry him—had stung. So he'd said what he'd thought she wanted to hear, except that she seemed to want something else. Something that must be impossible, something that *was* impossible to him because she seemed unable to make him understand what it was.

The most recent detailed explanation of what she wanted, he thought, was that she wanted a man who could talk about emotions. He thought they'd cleared that up.

Sean Devlin could talk about emotions, and Cameron did not want him. Cameron, Paul believed, wanted him, Paul.

But she seemed to want him to do some mysterious thing that was impossible to accomplish—because he had no idea what it was.

That evening, after a shower to wash off all the monkey smells, he drove to his father's house for dinner. His father lived next door to Graham Corbett, a fact that had caused Paul some irritation for months without Paul's consciously acknowledging the fact. He'd enjoyed teasing Cameron about Graham.

But then he'd begun to feel irritation over her preference for someone so…unworthy of her. Not that Graham was a bad guy. Perfect for Mary Anne, in fact. But Cameron deserved…

Better than me, Paul thought wryly. The thought lasted only briefly. Actually, though he didn't understand Cameron, he thought he probably understood her better than anyone else did. And he imagined she would be the first to admit that.

The real crux of the matter was that Paul found her fascinating and was suddenly very unwilling to cede her to anyone else.

His father had made spaghetti, which had always been his single-father staple and which he'd fed to Paul and Bridget during their visits with him. Thursday night dinners, just Paul and his father, had become a tradition when Paul was in his teens. Bridget and David had dined on Tuesday nights, but their day of the week had become more flexible over time.

The former obstetrician asked, "How's Cameron?"

"Fine, as far as I know. She went to Dr. Henderson today, but I haven't heard how it went." Paul suspected he was going to have to live down missing the appointment because of monkeys. "I hope he told her she has to have the baby in the hospital."

"Why?" his father asked, serving up the pasta and sauce and a side of bell peppers.

"Because her sister had a terrible birth after half a million miscarriages, and because Cameron is built just like her."

Paul was relieved that his father didn't downplay what seemed to Paul obvious dangers.

"What's she going to do after the baby is born?"

Paul gave him a blank look. "What do you mean?"

"She has a pretty demanding job." He nodded toward Paul's ear, which had not yet completely healed from the bite he'd received from the enraged husband at the Women's Resource Center. To Paul's satisfaction, after an emergency meeting of the board, a security guard had been hired for the facility.

"She'll probably keep working," Paul said. He hadn't given the issue any thought. In his imagination, he'd gotten as far as coming home from the zoo to Cameron's house and the baby. He could afford to buy a home, but it had never been a priority while renting was cheap, which it was. Perhaps if they outgrew Cameron's house…

If she lets you live there with her, Paul.

At the moment, that *if* yawned like a chasm.

His father did not look at him but said, "I suppose marriage bells would be too much to hope for."

"Why does everyone want us to get married?" Paul dug into the food irritably. He hated the way the question sounded. At the moment, he hated the whole topic.

"Because you've made a woman pregnant and children need two parents. You and Cameron have been friends for years, and marriage doesn't sound unmanageable for the two of you."

Paul said, "What about the marriage *you* abandoned twenty-five years ago? You and Mom have been friends for years, but marriage was obviously unmanageable for the two of you. Not to mention that you walked out on her at what was probably the worst time of her life." His accusations, to him, sounded a bit childish, but he felt almost unable to stop himself from uttering them.

His father simply didn't answer.

"One instance of infidelity," Paul continued, determined to get a reaction.

"The infidelity had little to do with it. It was the cover-up. I couldn't be party to it."

"You wanted her to have to fight?"

David Cureux sighed. "No. I wanted the issue to be dealt with correctly. Practicing midwifery without a license is a *misdemeanor.* The consequences wouldn't have been as extreme as your mother feared." He paused, seeming to consider the accuracy of the statement. "Her response was, in my opinion, wrong. And remember, this was my boss she made this deal with."

"You transferred," Paul remembered. "You went to work in—"

"Another county," his father finished. "Till he moved.

Which fortunately occurred a few years later." He hesitated. "I had little bitterness toward your mother. I understood her. But I couldn't stay, knowing what I knew."

"Surely you could have worked it out." Paul tried to imagine himself and Cameron involved in such a situation. It was difficult to imagine, but he believed he would stand by her in such a case.

His father shook his head. "Paul, I'm a physician. I went to medical school. I spent more than a decade of life training, becoming a physician and then an obstetrician and gynecologist. I paid malpractice insurance. Being a physician meant a great deal to me and still does. I had to distance myself from what they'd done to protect myself—and, I told myself, you and Bridget."

"You and Mom both chose your careers over your marriage."

"Probably because neither what she does nor what I did can be classed as a career. The correct word is vocation, and a vocation is a part of who a person is."

Paul shook his head. "And I suppose being a zookeeper doesn't qualify."

His father shook his head, not as a negative but as a refusal to address that assertion. He took a breath. "I believe that being a zookeeper is a vocation. It is a coveted job, and you've worked in several capacities as a zookeeper. You have meaningful interaction with your charges."

"It's fine, Dad," Paul murmured, laughing slightly. He knew himself to be fortunate that neither of his parents had ever tried to lead him into a particular line of work. They'd simply wanted him and Bridget to be happy.

"You don't respect my not marrying Cameron." Paul wasn't sure whether to tell his father that he'd extended the offer and been refused. He felt a quiet fury that his father should stand in judgment over him on an issue of marriage when his own marriage had collapsed.

His father seemed to consider. He shrugged. Said nothing.

Which was saying everything.

David brought a portion of spaghetti to his mouth. He swallowed, drank some water. "Bridget put one of her potions in your water glass at the restaurant."

Paul choked on the piece of bread he'd been swallowing. A love potion! That explained it. Suddenly, in the middle of dinner, he'd been overflowing with love for Cameron. His father had no faith in the love potions. Paul's faith in them was absolute. Time after time, he'd seen the people who'd drunk them end up married. He'd thought for a time that Mary Anne and Graham Corbett were the exception, thought Mary Anne had given a love potion to a different man. Wrong.

They always worked. There was no turning back from them. There was no antidote.

His father said, "If those things worked, you'd be begging Cameron to marry you."

"I *did* ask," Paul said.

His father frowned, heavy still-black eyebrows drawn down. "Well, that wasn't because of the love potion."

It was like David Cureux to focus on the inefficacy of love potions rather than on the fact that Paul had actually made an offer of marriage to Cameron and been refused.

"I don't think she thought I was sincere—or something. She told me to get out of the house."

His father looked up, obviously surprised by Cameron's reaction. "Were you sincere?"

"I meant it, if that's what you mean. Yes, I was sincere. I asked her, and if she'd said yes, we would be engaged and I would marry her."

"Well, I have no answer for you."

Paul felt some of his father's disapproval melt away. His coldness had changed to puzzlement, as though he, too, wondered why Cameron had refused Paul. He said, "I never would have suspected her of—" He stopped short, as though he feared saying too much.

"Being romantic?" asked Paul.

"Not exactly. But I've always found her to be an extremely pragmatic young woman."

Paul made a sound like a grunt. "The pragmatic woman who was irrationally terrified of childbirth and now wants a homebirth, who I think wants to marry me but said no, and who is now basically not talking to me." *And Bridget gave me a love potion.*

His father seemed to sense his thoughts. "You can't believe those things work. Their working would negate free will."

Paul considered whether the way he'd come to feel about Cameron was a product of free will. *I really began to feel this way before the restaurant.* For him, it had begun…

Back in college.

That one night. Glitter in his bed and a naked girl on his hands. It had seemed like too much. He hadn't wanted to deal with her emotions. But in some ways, he'd spent all the years since doing just that. She'd been his best friend. He'd teased her through crushes, tended her when she was sick, taken her dogs to the vet, rescued her again and again.

Have I been in love with her all this time?

"Things have a way of working out," his father told him philosophically.

Paul said nothing, just felt again the overwhelming responsibility of that baby coming.

Then his father suggested, "You must court her."

"I am! I took her to dinner. I brought her flowers."

David repeated, "I hope you don't put any faith in those potions. It's errant nonsense."

Paul wondered if giving *Cameron* a love potion would make any difference. But possibly Bridget had already given her one....

MEANWHILE, CAMERON SAT across from Sean at a new restaurant that had opened downtown. It offered a variety of ethnic cuisine—a plan that Cameron had noticed usually seemed to fail in restaurants. But the food here was all right. She'd gone with a Thai dish, while Sean had chosen Indian.

They talked about the play she was to see that night, about the challenges and joys of directing high school students. Sean said, "I love that they believe in their dreams. Their idealism hasn't been crushed."

Cameron remarked, "Are you saying that yours has?"

He shook his head. "Not mine. But other people seem to feel that maturity takes the edge off it. We get older and the dreams don't come true the way we thought they would. Maybe some people have an ability to always see the beauty in the way their dreams do come true. I don't know."

"Would you be one of those?" Cameron found herself thinking dismally of Paul. If he'd been one of her dreams, he definitely wasn't coming true in any way that she'd hoped.

He shrugged. "I know that I still have dreams. Plays I want to write. People I want to help. A woman I'd like to spend my life with."

Cameron's heart stopped. He couldn't mean her.

He seemed to sense her recoil. "Don't worry." He smiled. "That was saying too much. I go overboard sometimes. And it seems as though Paul is coming around. I know he's the one you really want to be with."

Cameron frowned. "It's not exactly that. I mean, yes, he is that person. And I *know* him, and he knows me, and there's complete comfort there. We've been best friends so long."

"Like Heathcliff and Cathy." Sean smiled.

"I wouldn't take *you* for a reader of romance."

"English was part of my major," he admitted, and Cameron thought how attractive and thoroughly *nice* he was. "I always remember her saying, 'Nellie, I *am* Heathcliff.' That seemed the essence of love to me."

"Have you had girlfriends since your divorce?" Cameron asked.

"One," he admitted. "I thought we had that kind of understanding. But she wasn't as much me as I thought, and I wasn't her. I fall in love rather easily."

"I believe that."

Cameron considered whether she could truly say, *I am Paul.* She thought, *No, thank God.* And yet there was that simple comfort of understanding each other, of knowing what the other would do in most circumstances.

But without completely *knowing* each other. Yes, she'd said that she knew Paul, and she believed she knew his heart, but there was so much she *didn't* know.

"Am I…" He seemed to begin, then stop. "Does my presence in your life cause problems between you and Paul?"

"No!" was her immediate response. If anything, it would do no harm for Paul to feel that he had a bit of competition. Then she told Sean about Paul's proposal and what she'd done. Sean was a trusted confidant and would not repeat the story to anyone. "Do you understand," she asked, "why I said no?"

"Yes," he replied without hesitation. "You feel he's—well, going through the motions is the best way I can put it."

Cameron nodded vigorously, stabbing a piece of chicken.

"Do you think he's afraid of intimacy?" Sean asked. "Emotionally, not physically."

Cameron considered. "I *used* to think that. He definitely doesn't like to sit around talking about his emotions. But—well, in some ways, he's very practical. In others, I feel like he'll never grow up. Maybe he's afraid of *commitment.* But despite that, he asked me to live with him and he asked me to marry him."

"It's not uncommon for men—and women—to fear commitment," Sean answered, as though this were a professional opinion. But he wasn't a professional in psychology, except as much as any actor-playwright-director-teacher. "They feel that to be in an adult relationship would make them grow up. It's a Peter Pan complex."

For the first time, Cameron didn't like Sean. She knew she herself sometimes compared Paul to Peter Pan, but she didn't care for anyone else to do so. Especially because—well, Paul *wasn't* so immature. As he'd said himself, many people thought it more mature *not* to rush into marriage. "He's a responsible person," she said.

Sean did not look skeptical. He said, "Sorry. Maybe a little of my own jealousy rearing its ugly head."

And peace was restored.

"THE DOCTOR SAID you're fine," Mary Anne reminded Cameron over the following week as she and Cameron helped clean up the face-painting area at the end of the winter solstice celebration at the zoo. Since Paul hadn't been able to make it to Dr. Henderson's office, Mary Anne had accompanied Cameron to her appointment. "And Clare says the same. I'm sure if both still feel it's safe when the time rolls around, when you go into labor, Paul will be on board, as well."

Mary Anne had come to Cameron's second prenatal appointment with the midwife, as well. Cameron had begun joking that when Paul couldn't make it to the birth because the monkeys had monkey pox, Mary Anne could come in his place.

"What about Sean?" Mary Anne had suggested.

Cameron hadn't answered.

Now, changing the subject from the birth, still months off, Cameron told Mary Anne all about Paul's proposal and her refusal.

"He probably thinks you're completely insane," Mary Anne decided. "He thinks you wanted to marry him until he asked, and then you changed your mind."

"Probably. But *you* understand why I said no, don't you?" Having asked this question first of Sean, Cameron now began to feel as though she were taking a poll—or perhaps simply trying to convince herself that she'd done the right thing.

"Yes," Mary Anne answered. "You want him to *want* to marry you, not to propose because he knows it's expected of him."

"Exactly."

"But are you sure that's what he's doing? Cameron, he may really want to marry you. People change, and you two are going through many big changes."

Cameron considered this. "I don't know anymore. I just know that I've been made to feel as though I'm *expecting* something of him, and he has an idea of the expectation, and now, maybe, he's acting on it." She glanced quickly behind her back. They were using a keeper area off the zoo hospital to rinse out paint trays, but so far they were alone.

"What would it look like," Mary Anne asked, "for him to behave as you'd like him to behave?"

Cameron considered this. "I suppose I'd like him to be in love with me."

"Cameron, maybe he is!" Mary Anne exclaimed.

But Cameron knew that the reason she'd told Paul to leave was because she'd known that he *wasn't* in love with her. But had asked her to marry him anyway.

At that moment, Paul pushed open the door to the zoo hospital.

She wished her heart wouldn't pound so fiercely every time she glimpsed his face.

"Ready to go?" he asked. He'd driven her to the zoo and planned to drive her home, as well.

Cameron nodded, looking at Mary Anne. They all walked out together, Paul locking the employee exit behind him. After Mary Anne had started her car and driven off, Cameron got into Paul's truck with him.

"What are you doing Christmas Eve?" he asked. "Do you have plans with your family?"

"I'm usually expected to show up." She thought for a moment. "Want to join me?" At her parents' house. Her grandmother was supposed to be there, the grandmother who hadn't yet been told that Cameron was pregnant. That was because Cameron was unmarried, and it was all supposed to be too much for Nanna.

Paul nodded. "I love Christmas at the McAllister house."

"Ha ha," said Cameron, knowing that he meant there might be family drama there to witness. Her uncle, Mary Anne's father, being drunk perhaps. Or simply the family collusion to keep everything unpleasant from Cameron's grandmother.

He said, "Thank you for inviting me. Of course, I'll join you."

She felt that strange comfort with him, that brotherly comradeship that crossed into something unknown and exciting. Best friends and more…. Was it possible that what Mary Anne had suggested could be true? Could he want to marry her for some reason beyond the baby?

Christmas Eve

WHEN SHE HEARD the knock at her door, Cameron thought it might be Paul, arriving early to drive her to her grandmother's. But when she opened the door, Sean stood there.

He was carrying a package wrapped in gold paper and tied with a ribbon. "Merry Christmas," he said, holding the gift toward her.

Cameron had bought one for him, too, a small journal which she'd had gift-wrapped at the store. She said, "Come on in," and went to pick it up from beside a foot-high artificial tree Mary Anne had given her one year when she was ill. Sean's wreath, hanging on the door, was larger than the little tree.

They sat down on her couch and each opened their gifts. Hers was a 1931 edition of *Wuthering Heights* illustrated with woodcuts. "This is beautiful, Sean. Thank you." She turned pages eagerly, looking at each representation of the characters, of scenes from the story.

"You're welcome." He lifted the journal slightly. "And this will come in handy."

Cameron heard the sound of a vehicle outside. "That will be Paul."

She stood and went to the door, opened it and looked out.

He was unloading a Christmas tree from his truck, while casting contemptuous looks at Sean's Volvo.

Sean, behind Cameron, said, "Let me see if he needs a hand."

THERE WASN'T TIME to more than put it in a stand Paul had brought and test the lights on the floor before the two of them had to leave for Cameron's parents' house. Sean left well before that time, no doubt sensing that his presence was unwelcome. When he was gone, Cameron said, "Paul, I don't have any Christmas ornaments."

"I thought we could make some. Maybe when we come back from your folks' house." He indicated a paper bag, which seemed to contain art supplies and other assorted junk. He looked from the copy of *Wuthering Heights* to Cameron's face. "Do you like him?"

"Just as a friend. I mean, he's a good-looking guy, but—" She shrugged, meaning to imply general indifference to whatever else Sean might have on offer.

"Does he know he's just a friend?" Paul asked.

"I've told him so."

"And he remains hopeful?"

"Maybe that's why he's hopeful," Cameron said, as though considering for the first time the possibility that Sean liked her because she was in love with another man.

"Which reinforces what I've told you before," Paul said. "You represent the unknown to him. But he is the known to you."

Cameron frowned. "But I don't know him as well as I

know you, for instance." And yet it was Paul who interested her, who intrigued her, who held her happiness in his hands.

Paul looked down, afraid to gaze at her, suddenly disturbed by how much he felt. He focused instead on the Christmas lights. After checking that every bulb had successfully lit, he pulled the plug from the wall. "Let's head out."

THOUGH CAMERON'S MOTHER had reacted stolidly to her pregnancy, Cameron's grandmother, with whom Mary Anne had lived pre-Graham, had still not been told. Mary Anne, following the family line, maintained that Jacqueline Billingham might die of shock hearing news of the out-of-wedlock pregnancy. Cameron knew better. Her grandmother would say, "My goodness," and then ignore the situation. It wasn't that Nanna believed such things could never happen in her family. She would just behave as though that were the case.

Jacqueline had been brought to the Christmas Eve dinner by her attendant, Lucille. After the meal, Jacqueline sat on the couch, admiring Cameron's parents' Christmas tree.

Paul sat near her, while Mary Anne's father plucked out tunes on the piano, and her mother listened attentively to the interests of Beatrice's four-year-old daughter.

When Cameron had told Paul that the family was still colluding to keep the pregnancy from her grandmother, she'd seen a mischievous, almost Peter Pan-like expression flit over his features. "Don't you dare," she'd whispered.

This wasn't because she thought her grandmother

shouldn't be told but because she didn't think Paul was the person to deliver the news. "We've got to tell her," Cameron said to her own mother in the privacy of the kitchen.

Beatrice, as elder sister, said, "Maybe put it off a little."

"You might miscarry," Cameron's mother pointed out.

Tears sprang behind Cameron's eyes.

"Oh, honey, what is it?" her mother exclaimed.

"You shouldn't have said that," snapped Beatrice, sensitive to Cameron's fears and fully realizing that their mother had just predicted that Cameron's child might die.

But neither of them said Cameron wouldn't miscarry.

Cameron fled to the bathroom, and a moment later Paul walked in without knocking. He lifted her from the edge of the bathtub, where she'd been sitting, holding her stomach as she cried.

He pressed his face to her hair. "You won't miscarry," he said. "It's okay. That won't happen." And he touched her stomach, too, as though seeing if he could feel any difference.

"It *could.*"

"Nope," he said, hugging her. "Won't happen."

Cameron thought, *Is it possible he understands? And is there a chance that the idea is as horrible to him as it is to me?*

A few minutes later, he led her back into the living room, and he resumed his seat beside Cameron's grandmother.

Jacqueline looked at Cameron in surprise. "Are you all right, dear?"

"Well, she's pregnant, so we're a little anxious some-times," Paul said blandly.

Jacqueline Billingham looked at him once, then admired the Christmas tree. "Don't those old ornaments look nice?"

"We hope you can come to our wedding," Paul continued.

Cameron's jaw dropped. The exclamations that occurred to her, *What wedding?* and *We're not getting married!* could not be spoken before Jacqueline Billingham.

"Of course I will," exclaimed Cameron's elegant grandmother. "When is the date?" she asked Cameron.

"Probably after the baby's born," Cameron replied blithely.

"Perhaps," Paul agreed. "But possibly sooner. We know how important it is to the baby."

Cameron wanted badly to contradict all this.

But having married parents *could* be important to their baby.

Wasn't this the point when she should cease to worry about her own feelings and start to think about her child's instead? She *loved* Paul, and her only doubts had to do with his real desire to marry.

"Though we were thinking of the first Saturday in January," she said sweetly, hoping to watch Paul's face pale.

She could detect no reaction at all.

"Just a small ceremony at the courthouse," Cameron added. "After all, Mary Anne's is the big wedding we're looking forward to." As Mary Anne entered the room with her fiancé, she said, "Mary Anne, how does the first

Saturday in January work for you? For Paul's and my wedding?"

Mary Anne pasted on a quick smile. "Great! But that's soon to get you a dress."

"I'm not having a dress," Cameron replied. "It's ridiculous. For me," she quickly added.

"I don't see why," Graham Corbett put in with that very nice manner that was the hallmark of all his behavior.

Cameron shrugged. "I'll find something."

Paul said, "I'm not sure that date will work. It's very soon." He met her eyes and said firmly, "You're going to have a *real* wedding, Cameron."

An hour later, back at her house, sitting at her kitchen table with them, both surrounded by art supplies and assorted junk he'd brought over for making ornaments for the tree, she asked, "How do you feel about the first Saturday in January?"

"I *feel*," he answered carefully, "that it's too soon."

"So that was just to save you from my family's disapproval?" she inquired.

"Was *what* just to save me from your family's disapproval?"

"Pretending we're engaged."

He lifted his eyes. He'd stopped at his place briefly, loading a few things under the truck's camper shell, before driving back to Cameron's. He looked back at what he was doing, pasting magazine photos onto a small origami box. He had already used Cameron's stepladder to string lights on the tree.

Finished, he stood from the table, walked into the

living room to retrieve something, returned to the kitchen. He set an old-fashioned ring box in front of Cameron.

Suddenly uneasy, she put down the candy cane she'd been turning into a reindeer and picked up the box. She met Paul's eyes.

He lifted his eyebrows slightly and picked up the origami box again.

Cameron opened the ring box and found it contained a diamond ring in an old-fashioned setting.

"It was my grandmother's. My father's mother."

Cameron realized she had misjudged him, perceiving that the engagement was just for the benefit of her family—or for hers, in their eyes.

She removed the ring from the box and tried it on.

"We can have it sized," he said.

"It fits." Good grief. She was really going to be married to Paul. Not next weekend, but…

"I have a gift for you, too."

She stood up and went to get his gift from the other room.

Paul unwrapped a new copy of *Spiritual Midwifery.*

He said, "I'm supposed to read this?"

Cameron gave him a small smile.

"And it will reconcile me to you giving birth at home? Have you forgotten that my mother is a midwife, that I grew up surrounded by the concept of homebirth, that I've been subject to indoctrination, if you will."

"So what's wrong with me having this baby at home?"

That I'm terrified, Paul reflected.

He realized the incredible. That he wasn't afraid of her losing the baby. He was afraid of losing *her*.

Which was irrational.

"Nothing," he finally said. "You know, that ring isn't your present. It's just your engagement ring. If you like it well enough. If you don't, we can pick out another."

"I like it."

"Shall I get your present? It's out in the truck."

"Okay." She was glad she had another present for him, as well.

He left her. When she heard the front door reopen, Paul called, "Close your eyes."

"Okay," she called back and obediently shut them.

She thought she heard Mariah whine. A moment later, something fluffy was in her hands, and she opened her eyes. A tiny, long-haired Russian blue kitten gazed up at her with eyes the color of its name. "Hello!" she exclaimed.

The kitten trembled, apparently not happy about the nearness of Mariah, who had come close to sniff it.

Then, abruptly, a tiny paw shot out, a claw hooking on a black nose.

Mariah yelped and backed away with her tail between her legs.

"Well done," Paul said. "He can take care of himself. What do you want to name him? After one of the heroes of those books you adore?"

"One of the classics," she decided. "Ethelbert. Bertie. From *Barchester Towers*."

Paul looked wondering.

"He's just silly and funny."

"It's a good name for a cat," Paul agreed. "I brought you a litter box, but you're not to touch it, got that? I'll be over here every day to take care of it."

"How did you know pregnant women are supposed to avoid them?"

"I just do," he answered. "*And* I know why."

"Yes, well, you work in a zoo, and I suppose zoo animals can get toxoplasmosis."

"Too often."

"Thank you for Bertie," Cameron said and set the kitten on the floor.

Mariah ran out of the room.

"She'll get used to him," Paul assured Cameron. "And I don't think she'll try to eat him."

"But her father might."

"Let's keep Bertie inside and Wolfie outside for the time being."

"Okay," Cameron agreed.

They hung their homemade ornaments on the tree, went to bed and made love. When Cameron awoke in the morning and went into the living room, she found another ornament on the tree, a Hallmark ornament with Charlie Brown and a Christmas tree.

Paul said, "I thought it could start a tradition. A new ornament every year."

Every year. The words, for Cameron, were the greatest gift of the day. He intended to be with her during all the Christmases to come.

CHAPTER TEN

February 13

PAUL WAS INVITED to Mary Anne and Graham's dinner on the eve of their wedding. He was invited as Cameron's date. Because Graham's dissertation advisor had been unable to come to the wedding and because Sean Devlin and Graham had become friends since Sean's move to Logan, it was Sean who would walk up the aisle beside maid-of-honor Cameron on the following day.

Paul bore this with civility. When Cameron told him that Sean would be best man, Paul simply said that seemed reasonable as he and Graham were very similar. Mary Anne maintained to Cameron that Paul had said that because he was jealous of both men.

As Paul sat beside Cameron at the long table, Graham spoke to him. "*You're* going to be the next to go through what I'm feeling right now."

Cameron grinned. "What *are* you feeling, Graham?"

"Terror and excitement," he told her with satisfaction.

"But you've been married before," she remarked, for Graham was a widower.

"Makes no difference," he said. "I've never been married to Mary Anne."

She wondered how she would feel if she and Paul had not become lovers and conceived a child together. Would she now feel envious of Mary Anne? Would she wish that she herself were to walk up the aisle beside Graham? If so, that would be, Cameron decided, a silly reaction. After all, she herself had never been on a date with Graham.

Paul and Cameron drove home from the dinner together, Paul stopping briefly at his rented house to collect a few boxes. He was gradually moving into Cameron's. In the morning, she would be going to her grandmother's house to help Mary Anne dress for the wedding. Cameron had always considered herself untraditional, never caring *if* she married. But suddenly she was extremely conscious of being pregnant and unmarried. While she certainly wasn't envious of Mary Anne, her own situation slightly depressed her.

She had become pregnant by someone she still didn't think was keen to marry her.

But we are engaged.

And the things he had done at Christmas were so thoughtful. A tree. A first ornament. His grandmother's ring. And Bertie.

The dress she put on for Mary Anne's wedding was one she and Mary Anne had chosen together. Neither were seamstresses, and they'd picked out a flowing dress with an empire waist. It was in fall colors, browns and rusts, and Cameron liked how she looked in it. With the pregnancy, her breasts had grown fuller and her abdomen had begun to round. The dress certainly did not hide the fact that she was pregnant, yet it was graceful.

Mary Anne planned to keep to the tradition of not allowing herself to be seen by the groom prior to the ceremony, and Sean Devlin was under strict orders to keep Graham (who lived around the block from Mary Anne's grandmother) well away from the bride.

It was while she was watching Mary Anne arrange her own hair—being better adapted to this task than Cameron—that Cameron first felt a slight cramping sensation. She thought nothing of it.

Mary Anne was beautiful in white satin. Her dress had capped sleeves and a sweetheart neckline. She and Cameron had both loved the veil, attached to a small cap, which only someone with Mary Anne's model's bones could wear. She was borrowing an old blue cameo belonging to their grandmother. It went well with Mary Anne's coloring, which was similar to Cameron's.

Cameron helped her fasten on the choker and told her, "You are so gorgeous. You *are* glowing. I really haven't seen you so beautiful."

"I'm so *happy*," Mary Anne whispered. "I know Graham and I are right for each other."

Cameron hugged her cousin from behind. "Wait till he sees you."

The doorbell rang and Lucille came up to say that Paul Cureux was downstairs.

Cameron went down to see him and thought again how fantastic he looked when he bothered to put on a suit. "What are you doing here?" she asked. "Is anything wrong?"

"I brought your corsage. Mary Anne's bouquet is at the church."

She clapped a hand to her forehead. She'd forgotten that Paul had offered to run flowers to their various locations.

Her corsage was made of orchids, and she said, "You pin it on," and he did a good job of it, then kissed her lips.

"By the way," he suggested, "you might want to catch that bouquet."

Cameron laughed.

Paul thought how beautiful she was, and later he did not mind seeing her go up the aisle with Sean as it was simply all part of the ceremony of Mary Anne's wedding. As he watched Cameron, he remembered hearing from his mother about the reasons for his parents' divorce. What his mother had done wasn't precisely even infidelity, as infidelity was a matter of the heart. Not that Paul considered things that way in his own life. But his mother had been coerced into sex. Had allowed herself to be? Had chosen to be? It was too murky to judge. In any case, his father hadn't left because of Clare's unfaithfulness—at least as Paul understood David Cureux's motives. It seemed to have more to do with personal integrity and, as in his mother's case, with career. Paul wished his mother hadn't done what she'd done. But how wrong people were to think his long reluctance to commit to a woman stemmed from issues about his parents' marriage. It never had.

His reasons had been entirely different. He'd not

wanted to see the end of an era in his life. Cameron's becoming pregnant marked the end of that era. When she became pregnant, moving forward had become inevitable. The birth of their child would end that former era far more effectively than matrimony could. He accepted that he was going to have to move into a new role.

Cameron glanced at Graham Corbett's face as he watched Mary Anne, truly a vision in white, come up the aisle. She saw him dash a tear from his eye, then smile broadly, obviously blissful, overwhelmed with happiness.

He's so in love with her, she thought.

Cameron tried to imagine Paul gazing at her like that, but she couldn't. He loved her, but she imagined that to him... Well, the wedding wouldn't be as emotional as it clearly was for both Graham and Mary Anne. She could see Paul showing satisfaction but not this, not a tear of happiness.

Later, as Cameron's date, Paul sat at the head table with the bridal party at the reception. Paul held her hand often as he sat beside her. He felt a comfort in touching her.

Cameron turned to him once or twice, and he gave her small, quiet smiles. There was something very intimate in his smiles. They spoke of something he shared only with her, a closeness that could belong to no one else. Cameron felt content in that feeling—that she was special to him, that the day-to-day business of living gave her a unique knowledge of Paul. With Paul, this was intimacy of the highest kind.

She had at times suspected Bridget had dosed *her* with a love potion. But that didn't matter. She had always loved Paul. What she'd felt for Graham had been infatuation with someone she really didn't know. Paul she knew, and no potion had been necessary, so whether Bridget's potion had been a love potion—and Cameron now leaned toward the notion that it had been what Bridget claimed, an elixir to restore emotional equilibrium—was moot.

Joining the two of them briefly at the table, Paul's sister lifted Cameron's left hand and observed, "That was made to go there." She glanced at her brother. "And you say love potions don't work."

Cameron started.

He said, "What goes around comes around, Bridget."

"I'm already happily married." And indeed, her husband Billy was across the room, with Merrill on his lap as he ate, Nick beside them, talking a mile a minute. Bridget caught Billy's eye and blew him a flirtatious kiss.

Cameron, however, was more interested in the undercurrent of Paul's and Bridget's exchange. She stared between the two of them, catching all the nuances of the conversation. As Bridget moved away, Cameron asked Paul, "Has she admitted to giving me a love potion? Were you behind that?"

He squinted at her as though puzzled, then touched his own chest. "She gave *me* a love potion."

History flashed through Cameron's mind. History preceding a long ago night when she'd first ended up in Paul's bed and in the morning… Paul's reaction when he first knew she was pregnant… Then…

"When?" she asked.

He shrugged. "The night you and I came here for dinner, I think. She and my father were here?"

Cameron was thunderstruck. Was his attention to her all down to the love potion?

And now we're engaged.

No free will.

Did she believe that? Paul had long been so opposed to marrying anyone ever. "Do you think the love potion worked?" she asked Paul quietly.

"No," he said. "I've always found you attractive, you've been my best friend for years, and now you're having my baby."

"*Our* baby," she corrected, slightly stung by his phrasing of the sentiment. "But you believe the potions work. You asked me to live with you after drinking it."

"Then maybe it made me see what I'd felt all along." He spoke rather casually but seemed to sense Cameron's frown, her uncertainty. He looked up, met her eyes. "Cameron, let it go. I'm happy. You're happy."

That was true. But Cameron couldn't quite let it go. She wished she felt more certain and was angry with herself for always wanting further displays of his commitment to her. She'd never thought of herself as insecure, yet ever since becoming lovers with Paul, ever since the night the baby was conceived, she'd felt nothing else—at least as regarded his feelings for her. She repeated, "But you've *always* believed that your mother's and sister's love potions work."

As she spoke, she felt a slight cramping in her

abdomen, like the onset of menstrual cramps. It took a moment to register, and when it did, she ceased to care about their conversation.

No.

And there was a warmth between her legs. She feared for her dress and instantly rose to go to the bathroom. But she was bleeding, knew she must be. She threw an anguished look toward Clare Cureux, across the room, but Clare was looking the other way. She heard Paul say, "Cameron, what is it? Are you all right?"

She kept walking, hurrying to the ladies' room, wondering what Paul would feel if she lost the baby, if he would feel trapped by the promises he'd made.

Or if, she thought glumly, the love potion Bridget had given him would prevent even that.

But she had little energy for worrying about losing Paul. The fear of losing the baby was too near and too real.

It wasn't a flow of blood, just spots, as at the beginning of her period. Still feeling cramped, she walked back into the dining room, found Clare and touched her shoulder. "I'm spotting."

BED REST and an infusion of herbs, which would help her to keep the baby if she was meant to keep it but which would not prevent her miscarrying a baby that was malformed or for some reason could not make it to term in her womb.

No lovemaking, either.

That was the plan.

From her bed, she heard the front door, and Paul came in, followed by Mariah and Wolfie. Wolfie, uncharacteristically, came within two feet of her and looked at her, as though concerned. The wild dog did not usually come close enough to people to be touched himself. Cameron knew that if she reached out to try to touch him he would retreat.

Paul set down a grocery bag on her rocking chair, left the room and returned with her television/DVD player, which usually lived, unnoticed, in the living room.

"What is it?" Cameron asked. She watched him take a DVD case from the grocery bag. She felt listless, couldn't bear to read anything but romances, couldn't face any book about pregnancy and birth. What if she was defective, could never carry a child to term? Clare had not been sanguine. *Bleeding this early*… And Cameron wanted, loved, *this* baby. This baby was not replaceable. A different baby would be…a different baby.

And what if there could not be any baby? she wondered again, panic-stricken.

"Bollywood," Paul said.

She frowned. She had heard of Bollywood but knew nothing about it.

"You don't know Bollywood?"

She shook her head.

"It's perfect for a confirmed romantic like you."

Cameron was soon engrossed in the story of a blind girl being wooed by an unconventional tour guide. Well, that was how it started.

Paul watched her. He rarely felt like praying, but he

felt like it now. Cameron wanted this baby, and he wanted Cameron's happiness. And if she miscarried, where would that leave them? Would she still want to marry him?

Would he still want to marry her?

Yes.

How strange that he felt certain of that. Though he believed love potions worked, he could not attribute this change of sentiment within himself to whatever Bridget had put in his water.

He watched the film with Cameron until his cell phone rang.

Cameron glanced at him as he answered and saw a stillness cross his face, a stillness that meant something bad had happened.

"They need a shooting team," he said. "If no one can dart him, you have to shoot him."

Cameron watched him listen to what was being said on the other end of the line. "I'll come," he finally said. "I don't know if the zoo can take him, and if we can it will only be temporary, probably. We don't have room in our collections for that. The director needs to make those decisions. Right."

He closed his phone and looked at Cameron. "Pet baboon."

Her brow furrowed. "Where?"

"Right here in Logan County," he replied. "The owner is a new resident, apparently. The cute baby named *Precious* has reached adulthood and is being uncooperative. Imagine that."

"You're not telling me something," Cameron said.

"Someone's been hurt," he said. That was undoubtedly the short version.

Paul remembered Cameron's being near the zoo when the zoo's chimps had been out. His fear for her.

"Be careful," she said.

"The police have the area cordoned off, it sounds like."

"Why would anyone do that?" she asked. "Have a baboon for a pet?"

"Ignorance," he answered. "They're cute when they're babies. But they grow up and don't get along in human households. They're wild animals, and they need a safe and appropriate environment. And a lot of people don't understand how strong they'll be as adults. Arms, jaws, any of it."

He kissed her before he left.

Clare had suggested *trying* two days of bed rest. If the bleeding stopped, she could get up again.

The bleeding *had* stopped, and Cameron thought she would get up for a while after the movie. She thought of her fierce desire for a homebirth, and now that seemed childish. Well, not childish perhaps, but certainly unrealistic in her case. She just wanted a healthy baby.

Her rationale had been that if she had the baby at home, she would be able to walk around, allowing gravity to help the baby come out. In the hospital, she felt certain, she would have to have an electronic fetal monitor, tying her to the bed, forcing her to remain on her back. The thought of being pressured to submit to the hospital routine had infuriated her, made her feel an intense fear of violation.

Now she only wanted the baby to survive, to be healthy.

Baby, stay with me, she thought. *We can do this.*

The movie had begun romantically, but it turned out that the hero was a terrorist. There were lots of special-forces-type scenes, and she realized it was not going to have a happy ending. Nonetheless, she liked it and felt thankful to Paul for introducing her to something new. She was in love with him, loved everything about him, and she didn't want to think about the love potion Bridget had given him or if he loved her only because of it.

When the movie was over, she called his cell phone.

"Hello?"

"Where are you?" she asked.

"Outside the cordon. They darted him, and he did go down."

"Did you realize that you brought me a movie about an innocent girl who falls in love with someone she doesn't know is a terrorist and who she then thinks dies but he doesn't, and they have a baby and she has to shoot him to save the people of India from being blown up?"

"Didn't you like it?"

"Actually, I did."

"Romance," he said, "can be about honor."

"I did like it," she repeated. "And you're right. It can be. It was romantic. You could tell he was really torn; he'd been indoctrinated by his grandfather. And he was afraid for the woman and the child." The words she'd spoken rippled through her with an eerie resonance. She sensed that Paul felt protective, fearful, for her and their baby.

Quickly pushing her own thoughts from grim outcomes, she asked, "What's going to happen to the baboon?"

"Well, there are two."

"Really?"

"This adult male and an infant that the owner is willing to part with because of what happened here."

Obviously, whatever had happened had been horrible. Cameron didn't ask. Instead she said, "Are they going to the zoo?"

"For right now, they are. It wasn't my decision."

"Is there no space?"

"And there are no other baboons. It's crazy. It's not even a mother and baby, though the owners claim the adult likes the baby. If it's true—well, that could be good. But he could kill it, too. They're like that."

"I'd like to see the baby."

"You'll probably get to. People are so stupid," he said, as though to himself. "This couple couldn't have kids, so—"

"It does make people crazy sometimes," Cameron replied, desperately afraid that *she* might become one of those people. Not that she would adopt a monkey or ape, but…

"I've got to go," he said.

"WE'LL KEEP HIM in the hospital."

Paul was furious. The zoo director had made the decision so as to create a "favorable impression" of the zoo.

"We're not a rescue facility for animals people shouldn't keep as pets, sir." Paul was holding the baby baboon and talking on the phone while the zoo vet and head curator, following the director's instructions, were loading the unconscious, overweight pet baboon, who had just permanently disfigured his keeper, into a van to take him to the zoo. "What's going to happen to them in the long run?"

"We don't have any baboons," the director responded, as though their acquiring two in this way was a good thing.

"But they're social animals! They need a group. And what about quarantine?"

"I've spoken with the vet," said the director calmly.

Finally, Paul closed his phone and joined the others at the van, giving the baby, with its distinctive smell, with its warmth and soft hair, to the vet. The things were really cute; he already felt attached to this one after simply holding it. But they should never be pets, for anyone anywhere.

It was dark when he returned to Cameron's house, and he found her in the kitchen, cooking dinner.

He said, "You're up."

"Yes. I need to go back to work tomorrow if I can." She did not want to lose her job. She'd been instrumental in building the Women's Resource Center into what it was.

"It seems more important," he said, "to keep from having a miscarriage."

She repeated what his mother had told her. Then she said, "I don't *want* to lose the baby. I'm terrified of losing the baby. But your mother did not think bed rest would stop me miscarrying at this stage. I know that we're only engaged *because* of the baby—and because your sister gave you a love potion."

He said, "You won't lose the baby."

She was eating almonds as she cooked, adding them to a pot of rice, steaming vegetables, creating the kind of healthful meal they both liked.

Changing the subject, he said, "So can we make love yet?"

She shook her head but was soothed by his asking. She noticed he hadn't denied either of her last two statements, so she repeated them. "Because I'm pregnant and because of Bridget's interference, you asked me to marry you."

"Fine," he said. "What's your excuse?"

She couldn't say with truth that it was the same. She'd become engaged to him because she was in love with him, and she definitely *wasn't* in love with him because of a love potion.

Paul crossed to the sink where she stood, took one of her hands and turned her to face him. He looked into her eyes and tried to remember everything useful he'd ever heard about being charming to women. Be truthful? Act like she's the only woman you've ever loved? Let her know that you're her slave? Actually, all of those things seemed rather easy, because, in some way, each was true. But none of them were what he wanted to express.

Those brown eyes in her small face cut into his heart. "It doesn't matter," he said, "about the baby. Or whatever reason I asked you to marry me. I'm glad we're engaged. I'm glad you're going to be my wife. You want to have this baby, and I want you to, and all of that's great, but it has nothing to do with why I love you or how I love you.

"Cameron, I just left a couple—well, the wife—the husband had been mauled—who were so determined to give their love to some helpless infantile creature that they adopted one—no, two—of a wild species." He felt like crying when he thought of it. "*Stolen* from its own mother. Cameron, I want to be with *you*. I didn't ask to marry the baby."

She pressed herself close to him, and he wrapped both arms around her and hugged her and stroked her bright hair in its two long braids.

CHAPTER ELEVEN

CAMERON RETURNED TO WORK the following day and worked the following week while Mary Anne and Graham were away on their honeymoon. They'd gone somewhere leaving from New York, their destination a secret even to Mary Anne. The height of romance. Well, assuming that Graham could be counted on to choose a romantic destination, which Cameron believed he could be. When Mary Anne called her to say they'd come home, it was to announce a fabulous time on one of the Virgin Islands.

Yes, indeed, it had been romantic.

Cameron considered the fact that Graham Corbett had drunk a love potion, and now he and Mary Anne were married. Yes, but Graham was definitely a case of a person who'd been smitten long before he drank the love potion. If Mary Anne had received one, well, that would matter, because for a long time Mary Anne had detested Graham, or at least claimed to.

But Paul....

She sat at her desk thinking of these things, glad, as she had been every day that week, that she was having no cramps, seemed just fine. A volunteer—Angie Workman, in fact, who'd been trained only in the last two weeks—popped her head in Cameron's office.

"There was a bad one, Cameron."

No one else was in the building but the security guard, and Cameron motioned for Angie to come in and shut the door.

"She thinks he's going to kill her, but she says if she goes to a safe house, even with the kids, she's sure he'll get them in the divorce because he's got a good job. I told her that legal aid could help her, but she said they wouldn't because she's had a DUI, though supposedly she's on the wagon now."

Cameron said, "It sounds like you did what you could. You just have to let it go. And she's right that the DUI will be a problem—how much, I can't say. It depends on the judge."

Angie sank into a chair. "I never want to get married. I thought I did." She'd been recently engaged, to the manager of the local radio station, whom Mary Anne had liked before she fell in love with Graham. *And before Graham drank a love potion.*

Cameron tried to get the love potion Paul had drunk out of her head, out of her thoughts. "But I'm so shocked that somebody who seems like a nice guy can turn into an animal."

"I think you have to know the person for a long time," she told Angie. "Sometimes people marry quickly, or they ignore signs, problems. Quick courtship is very typical in—well, the kind of relationships we see in here, the bad ones, I mean. You know, a guy who comes on very romantically, very fast..." Cameron found herself remembering again what Paul had told her, that by wanting him to talk about his emotions to her, she was expecting him to behave like a woman rather than like a man. She wondered if she had also wanted a very sudden romantic courtship. She didn't think so.

What she did know was that she loved Paul, that Paul was exactly the man she wanted. Perhaps he'd been right that she was attracted to him, in part, because he *didn't* tell her everything he was thinking and feeling. It was certainly true that Sean did tend to do this.

Angie gazed briefly at Cameron's left hand. "You're engaged. But yours wasn't a quick courtship. You've known Paul and known him for years."

"Yes," Cameron agreed, again banishing the love potion from her thoughts, "we've certainly known each other for a long time."

Her cell phone rang and she looked at the number displayed on the screen. Sean.

She opened her phone. "Hi."

Angie waved and left Cameron's office to return to the hotline.

"Hello," Sean said. "How's it going?"

Sean had called less frequently since Cameron had become engaged to Paul, and she hadn't heard from him since Mary Anne and Graham's wedding.

"I'm at work," Cameron said. "And so far, so good." Sean knew that she'd been spotting. Paul had taken to calling him "Uncle Sean," a wry reflection that Sean seemed as interested in the baby's well-being as Paul himself was.

"So everything's better?" Sean said.

"Yes," Cameron answered.

"And between you and Paul?"

"Great!" she said, not wanting Sean to have any hope that Cameron and he would end up together. But Sean was a good person to share worries with, because he listened and gave intelligent answers. "Sean, suppose there was such a thing as a love potion that worked. And say that you were in a relationship and found out that the person who you thought loved you for yourself had been given a love potion."

"Ah, the love potions," Sean remarked. Cameron decided he must have heard about the Cureux family potions from Mary Anne or Graham.

"Yes," Cameron said. "Wouldn't you feel as though your partner had been tricked, as though your relationship wasn't quite the real thing?"

"Did someone give Paul a love potion?" Sean asked, a smile in his voice.

"*Yes*. His sister."

"Break off the engagement, by all means," Sean replied. "You're right. His feelings for you can't be real. Find yourself a man who loves you *without* the benefit of a love potion."

Cameron understood his flirting and smiled in spite of herself. "Be serious," she said.

"I think it's less important whether a love potion is involved," Sean answered, "than that the kind of love between two people is lasting and is going to allow both of them to grow. That there will be a real partnership between them. After all, there's no proof that these love potions do anything. The only thing definitely real is the relationship between the two people."

"But Paul *believes* in the love potions, Sean. He believes so firmly and entirely that for him the thing has to work."

"Not your problem," Sean said succinctly. "But it's the last time I'm saying so. Believe me, if it's possible to break up the two of you, I'm happy to help make that happen."

"It would make no difference," Cameron said as gently as she could.

"You mean, you still wouldn't be over him? Or that your breaking up with Paul wouldn't guarantee your ending up with me? The last is certainly true, but it would give me a better chance. At the moment, you're unavailable."

"Do you think that might be the basis of your attraction to me?" Cameron asked, smiling again.

"Not the basis. But," Sean admitted, "it does add a certain piquancy to my feelings."

The phone on her desk rang.

"I've got to go," she told him. He quickly asked her if she could meet for coffee—in her case, tea—the following day, and she agreed. Then, she answered the other phone.

Mary Anne said, "Oh, my God, Cameron, did you hear about Billy?"

Cameron knew only one Billy whom Mary Anne could mean—Bridget's husband, Billy Marten.

"No," said Cameron.

"Oh, God," Mary Anne repeated. "Um, forget it."

"Forget what?"

"Wait. My editor's here." Mary Anne seemed to be at the newspaper, where she worked. "I've got to go."

"But what—"

Mary Anne, however, was gone.

Cameron punched the speed dial for Paul into her cell phone.

He didn't answer. She left a voice mail message. "Mary Anne just told me something happened to Billy, but she didn't say what."

Her heart thudded hard. Mary Anne hadn't wanted to tell her. Why? What was so bad that…

Her mobile rang a minute later. Paul.

She answered and asked if he'd received her message.

He said, "No, I was calling to tell you something. Something bad."

Bridget's husband, Billy, had been killed in a car accident. Paul's father had just called to tell him, and Paul had called to tell Cameron so that she wouldn't hear it from anyone else. Mary Anne must have heard about it on the police scanner at the newspaper or in some related way.

Cameron felt the shock go through her. She didn't know Billy well, certainly not as well as she knew Bridget. She knew that he worked hard. He'd been a contractor, had always had projects going, had always had too much work to do. But Bridget… "Where's Bridget? And the kids?"

"At my mom's. I'm going over there now. Shall I pick you up after work?" She'd been riding her bike to work as often as possible, but Paul was always willing to pick up her and her bicycle if she was tired at the end of the day.

"Thank you."

PAUL ALMOST DIDN'T recognize Bridget when he saw her. She had cut off her dreadlocks, and hers definitely looked like a homemade haircut, boyish. Her hair was as dark as his, though her dreadlocks had been bleached, lightened. Now, she looked like his twin. She sat on his mother's porch with her daughter, Merrill, on her lap, hugging her, while Nick sat on the porch swing with Paul's mother, rocking.

Paul climbed out of the truck, walked to the porch and sat down beside his sister, embracing her. Her face was tearstained. She said, "Look at this," and showed him a plant budding beside the porch step. "It's spring again."

Paul nodded, remembering how recently his sister had told him that she was happily married. It had been at Graham and Mary Anne's wedding. And undoubtedly she and Billy had danced there together, though he hadn't been there to see it. He and his mother and Cameron had left to get Cameron to her bed.

"I'm so sorry, Bridget," he said. "Where is he?"

"The funeral home. He wanted to be cremated. I thought we should both be cremated. But I think it's too traumatic for the kids."

Merrill, only two, seemed barely to comprehend any of it.

"Have you been down there?" he asked.

She nodded and began to cry again.

Nicky began to cry, too, and said, "I want Daddy." Paul knew that his nephew had a tendency to draw attention to himself in any crisis. Though Paul didn't negate the possibility that Nicky did want his father and did understand the concept of death, he suspected the boy might be more upset at seeing Bridget cry.

Paul set his nephew on his own knees and said, "Did you know we have a baby baboon at the zoo?"

The distraction worked.

"At the zoo?" Nick asked.

"Her name is Girl," Paul told him. "And there's an adult baboon named Precious, and he takes care of Girl."

"How?" asked Nick.

Paul felt torn between the need to continue distracting his nephew and to show sympathy for his sister. Then there were his own feelings about Billy, whom he'd liked.

And the situation he'd left behind at the zoo.

Situation one was the baboons—their temporary housing and the director's plan to build an exhibit for them.

Situation two was, for Paul, more worrisome. The sakis had produced a baby, and at first the mother had cared for her well. But then she'd seemed to notice that the male preferred pulling hairs from his tail to attending at all to her or the baby, and Paul constantly feared that, in what he perceived as her depression, she might abandon the infant.

Paul asked Bridget, "What can I do? Do you want the kids to stay with Cameron and me tonight?"

She shook her head emphatically, and he sensed that, in light of Billy's death, having the children close to her was more important than ever.

Clare said, "Nick and Merrill, let's go roll the piecrust."

She took the children inside, leaving Paul alone with his sister.

She said, through tears, "You know, when you're married, you sometimes get so mad at the other person. Sometimes you almost wish—well, wish they were gone. Or different. Or—"

"I doubt you have anything to feel guilty about, Bridget."

"*Everyone* has things to feel guilty about. But no—I mean, before he'd leave, always, I'd *always* tell him I loved him, and I'd *always* tell him to be careful. Well, also, he's the breadwinner."

"Are you going to be okay? For money? I mean, just now."

"Oh, I'll be fine that way. He was great at making money."

His phone rang, and Paul pulled it out to glance at the number.

The Women's Resource Center.

He answered.

Cameron said, "Paul, can you come and get me? I'm spotting again."

BRIDGET CAME WITH HIM to get Cameron, leaving Nick and Merrill with her mother.

Bridget and Cameron embraced as soon as they saw each other.

Cameron rubbed Bridget's new hair, held her tightly, said, "I think I'm supposed to lie down."

"Yes, that's the most important thing, and I brought herbs from Mom," Bridget said.

"You have other things to think about."

Bridget shook her head. "I have to do something. I have to have something to do. I can't stand it. I don't know what I'm going to do. But you're going to lie down in the backseat on the way home."

Cameron stretched out on the backseat of the dual cab, and Paul drove slowly back to her house. Inside, while she got into bed, Bridget prepared herbs in the kitchen and Bertie jumped up on the bed with Cameron. Mariah joined them, keeping her distance from the kitten, whom she still distrusted.

Bridget brought in an infusion for Cameron and pulled the rocking chair over to the bedside. Her face was pale, grief-stricken, and yet she seemed entirely focused on Cameron and on being a midwife. Paul stood in the doorway, and Bridget said, "Join us, will you?"

Paul came over and sat gently on the edge of the bed, taking Cameron's hand.

"Bed rest," Bridget said. "And we're going to get you in to see Dr. Henderson again, but we're pretty sure he will advise the same thing. Bed rest."

"Just for a few more days?" Cameron asked.

Bridget shook her head. "Probably," she said, "for the rest of your pregnancy. Beatrice did that, didn't she, before Trinity was born?"

Cameron nodded. Beatrice had also gone through bed rest several times and subsequently lost babies.

"Bed rest means you get out of the bed to go to the

bathroom and—when Paul's not here—to get food. Not to prepare food, but to get food out of the fridge and bring back to bed. You take baths, not showers, and the water needs to be tepid. Max is a hundred and one degrees—absolutely no higher than that."

Cameron had a horror of how dirty her house would become with her confined to bed. And what if Paul didn't want to cook for five more months? She looked at him anxiously.

He said, "I'll do the cooking."

"And we can get help for you, with the housework," Bridget said. "If you have insurance through your work—"

"I'll *lose* my job."

"Unlikely. Don't you have a second-in-command?"

Cameron nodded again, thinking of the fiftyish woman with a master's degree in sociology who was waiting in the wings, ready to take over her job. She felt like crying. She needed to be active; she went running or biking every day. How was she going to stand this?

But then she looked into Bridget's face, drawn, remembered that this widow would be going home tonight for the first time to a house without her husband—well, to a house her husband would never enter again. For many of Billy's jobs had been out of town. It hadn't been uncommon for him to be gone for five days at a time.

"Okay," she said. "Bridget, do you and the kids want to stay here tonight?"

Bridget shook her head. "We have to go back home sometime. I don't even know what Merrill understands.

Nick gets it a little better, but— It's best for us to go home. Mom said she'd come and spend the night with us if we want."

Paul said, "I better get started on dinner. Is there anything else you need to tell me, Bridget? About this? Cameron's bed rest, et cetera?"

"Tons," Bridget said, "but you've got the basic idea."

DURING THE NEXT TWO MONTHS, Cameron learned to be still—well, to exist without running, cycling and her usual active lifestyle and to be thankful in the expectation of resuming her past activities after the baby was born. *God, to be confined like this every day.* It wasn't that she'd never thought of the plight of disabled women—she saw them occasionally in the Women's Resource Center—but forced inactivity was a new experience.

Paul kept her supplied with all the Bollywood movies he could find and had even taken to browsing thrift stores for vintage romance novels he thought would fit her specifications.

Cameron still felt some concern that his decision to marry her had been caused by her pregnancy and a love potion, but she was dependent on him, and she felt a deep gratitude for everything he did for her. For so long, she'd called him immature, but he was not. He was reliable, responsible.

The zoo director was busy with the construction of a baboon exhibit and with acquiring other baboons to introduce to Precious and Girl, but Paul continued to worry about the sakis. Precious's owner had made national news because of her spouse being mauled. She and the injured spouse were on tabloid covers, and Cameron had learned more about the attack on the news. Because of the severe injuries to the owner, people were calling for Precious to be destroyed. The zoo was now keen to protect the baboon. Paul had been interviewed and said, "Nonhuman primates are wild animals. No baboon is made for cul-de-sac life. We're not going to destroy this baboon for being a baboon."

A Morgantown-based animal rights group, West Virginians for Animal Welfare, or WVAW, felt that Precious should be returned to his native land. "Nebraska?" Dr. Bannister had roared down the phone. "He was born at an illegal breeding operation in northern Nebraska. What makes you think he'd be happier there?" The keepers and zoo vet had chipped in on a bottle of Ardbeg, the director's favorite single malt, to show their support for this sound bite.

Paul had also been followed home by some WVAW members, who tried to enlist him in a plan to send the baboon to Ethiopia. They had ended up calling him names and accusing him of participating in "unethical husbandry practices."

One day when Paul returned from work, Cameron had exclaimed, "I felt the baby move." But Paul could not feel those movements from the outside till several weeks later. Cameron thought she would never forget his lying beside her, his hand on the rounded melon of her baby, the look on his face one of awe as he felt the baby move inside her.

Bridget and her children spent a fair amount of time at Cameron's house, usually appearing in the late afternoon when Nick and Merrill would "help" their mother with some housework. Cameron felt a gratitude for what she knew she could never repay. Bridget was subdued and very thin—"not hungry." Billy had been buried at a local cemetery, and she and the children took flowers to his grave daily.

Sean visited often after school and sometimes met Bridget at the house. When they were there at the same time, he often ended up playing with Bridget's children, and on May Day he helped them construct a maypole in Cameron's tiny backyard. Cameron watched through the window as the four of them danced around it and thought it would be nice if Sean would fall for Bridget and Bridget for Sean, but that didn't seem to be happening.

The baby was growing at a normal rate, and the bed rest had allowed her to hold on to the baby for twenty-eight weeks, well into viability.

Cameron had stopped reading about homebirths. She'd had a dream of the birth going a particular way, her laboring at home, perhaps enduring the worst pain of her life but triumphing, making her way through it, giving birth vaginally. Now her best hope was to give birth vaginally in the hospital.

She had to sleep almost sitting up because she had such trouble with gastric reflux. Whenever she got out of bed, it was difficult. She had to move carefully and had to hold up her belly, hold her child, as she waddled to the bathroom. Baths were tepid, showers nonexistent.

Cameron still longed to give birth vaginally, still thought about it a great deal. It seemed an empowering thing to push the baby out. If she had a cesarean section, someone else would be doing all the work. She wanted to do what women had been doing for thousands of years. She felt as though giving birth vaginally would give her greater strength—as a parent and also in her work with abused women.

Sean came inside through the back door and walked into the bedroom through her open door. He smiled when he saw her, the smile that always intensified his good looks. "Did you watch our maypole dance?"

"Of course. I loved it." She hesitated. "It's really nice for Bridget and her kids to get to be with you. You know. Because of Billy." She felt a need continually to impress upon Sean that to her he was a friend and could not be more. She wished he would fall for someone else—Bridget, for instance, not that Bridget was ready for romance. She was mourning Billy.

"They're great kids," Sean said matter-of-factly and sat down in her rocker. "How's baby McAllister-Cureux?"

"Not active just now. He was bumping around a little while ago."

"He?"

Though Cameron had allowed an ultrasound some weeks before, she had chosen not to be told the baby's sex.

"Or she," she answered.

"Have you thought of names?"

She shrugged. She and Paul had talked of names in a casual way. "I like Gabriela if we have a girl. We both do. We're not sure about boys' names."

Sean looked toward the front of the house just as Mariah stood up from her bed and Bertie jumped off the bed, both going to welcome Paul home. "Speak of the devil." Sean stood. "I'll make myself scarce."

"Thanks for coming by," Cameron told him.

She heard him greeting Paul as one man went out and the other came in.

Paul came to the bedside and kissed her. "I learned about something interesting today."

"What?"

"My father told me about it. He read about it, and apparently there's a new proponent of it at the hospital. It's called kangaroo care. For taking care of premature infants. You wear them against your skin—kind of like a baby kangaroo in its pouch. You know, around the hospital. Or wherever preemies are allowed to be at the hospital."

"Only in the Neonatal Intensive Care Unit," Cameron told him. "And I hope this baby *isn't* premature," she added fiercely.

"We both hope that. But I thought you'd want to know."

"Yes," Cameron agreed. Paul looked tired. She asked him about his day, wishing she could be the one to make dinner, to do something useful to make his life easier.

"How was the movie?" He looked at her most recent Bollywood offering, the box lying beside her on the bed.

"The guy is sooo immature. I'm not through with it. I'm hoping he'll improve or show a different side to his character. But he's just—adolescent."

"Like me?" Paul asked, a touch of asperity in his tone.

Cameron could not remember the last time she'd called him immature—or thought that he was. "Not remotely." She added, "You're not immature."

Paul smiled, but still there was a faint archness in the look.

"What?" Cameron said.

"I've heard rumors about my Peter Pan complex."

Cameron tried to remember if she'd ever said out loud to anyone that Paul had a Peter Pan complex. She remembered a conversation with Sean on the subject, but wasn't it Sean who'd used that expression? Had she *ever* used it?

She said, "I'm not sure I've ever said that about you. Where did you hear such a rumor?"

He gave it some thought. "Bridget?"

Had Sean been talking to Bridget about things Cameron had told him?

She decided to say, "Sean's been nice, playing with her kids."

"Yes, I'm sure that's why he comes over."

Cameron looked at him worriedly. "You're not jealous, are you?"

He seemed to consider. "I don't think I am. I don't think you're attracted to him. I suppose I think *he'd* be happier directing his attention elsewhere."

Paul was preoccupied. There were things he would

have liked to tell Cameron under other circumstances, things having nothing to do with Sean Devlin. But she was pregnant, trying not to miscarry.

He'd found a note on his windshield from the animal rights group that had been besieging him and other zoo employees. HOW WOULD YOU LIKE TO SPEND YOUR LIFE IN A CAGE?

It was a disturbing suggestion, threatening, and he'd considered taking it to the police but just stuck it in the glove box of the truck instead. He understood healthy activism. When he'd lived in England for a year, he'd joined the clown army to protest his own country's involvement in a war he believed pointless. But the animal rights activists objecting to the zoo holding Precious and Girl and caring for them seemed a few cards short of a full deck. He'd asked one of them, "Do you have the slightest idea what would be involved in sending a baboon to Ethiopia? Are you going to buy him a seat on a jet?"

The activist had said, "He's fairly docile normally, isn't he?"

Did this person read the news? Paul had then inquired.

Yes, but *we* want to return him to the wild.

Right.

Cameron seemed almost to guess his thoughts. "Heard any more from the weirdos?"

"Oh, yeah," Paul answered vaguely. "They're still at it."

She eyed him thoughtfully. She said, "Thank you for everything you're doing." She said it every day. Lovemaking—well, intercourse—was out of the question, though he slept with her, and they caressed each other in the night. Cameron wanted to somehow repay him for everything he was doing for her, and she had no idea how to accomplish that.

"You're welcome," he said. He stretched out on the bed and put his hand on her stomach, reaching under her maternity top.

The baby kicked within her, as though sensing his presence.

"Just woke up," Cameron said. "He must want to say hi. Have you thought of boys' names yet?"

He shook his head. "But we're not going to name him Precious."

She laughed. "Okay." Then, "What about William? Billy?"

Paul's breath caught a little. He mourned the loss of his brother-in-law, who had been a remarkable man, a good parent. Bridget had told him, *I was so lucky. I'm never going to find anyone half that good again.*

"That's a nice thought," he said. "I like it. If you do."

"I do. William is a nice name. We don't even have to call him Billy. Maybe Will."

"It's a good name."

He thought again of the rather too-frequent experience of coming home to find Sean Devlin leaving. Paul didn't think of himself as a jealous man, and he couldn't really imagine Cameron being unfaithful. But he wished Sean would make himself scarce—for his own sake. The guy was obviously head over heels in love with Cameron, but

Cameron was his, Paul's, fiancée. Though Paul didn't fear Cameron's falling for Sean, Paul sometimes had the unpleasant feeling that Sean was waiting for everything to collapse.

Nothing was going to collapse just now. Cameron needed him. That thought made Paul feel slightly guilty, as though he were binding her to himself with his own caretaking. But what else was he supposed to do?

He studied her. "You're okay…with us…aren't you?"

She looked startled, then almost pleased. "Why are you asking?"

"Because you sort of can't get along without me right now, and I don't want you to feel…captive."

HOW WOULD YOU LIKE TO SPEND YOUR LIFE IN A CAGE? Uneasily, he remembered the note.

"I feel a bit captive because I can't get out of bed except to go to the bathroom and take a bath. If you mean captured by you, I don't feel that way. If you're asking if I would still love you if I didn't need you right now, I would. Very much so."

Paul leaned over, held her, kissed her lips, stroked her hair. He said the words he seldom said. "I love you, Cameron."

"Pity Bridget had to give you a potion to make it happen."

He shook his head. "Don't be silly. I loved you when I made love with you. I probably loved you before that. I suspect I've been resisting you for some time."

"You didn't love me the first time we were together," she said, remembering the Halloween night and the morning after. "And I really liked you. Loved you. For a little while, I thought I was in love with you. But you didn't want me."

"That's wrong. I did and said what I did because I wanted your friendship, wanted nothing to be ruined. It's taken years of being your friend for me to see that we can be friends *and* lovers. Partners, if you will."

He did not say husband and wife, and Cameron sensed that the final union between them, the marrying, was still something he wanted to hold off, to put off.

Well, she was in no shape for a wedding.

Oh, to be able to go for a run. To ride her bike.

The baby kicked again, and she placed her hand on her abdomen.

Paul touched her full breasts through her top, reached beneath to touch her nipples, to rub them as books recommended, to prepare her for nursing. Stroked her smooth stomach.

Cameron had been propped up with a pillow. Now, she lay down beside him, caressing his face, unbuttoning his jeans, kissing him.

Content.

CHAPTER TWELVE

IN THE LAST WEEK OF MAY, Paul left work when it was still light. The days were getting longer. It had been a good day, preparing for tomorrow's arrival of two baboons who would join Precious and Girl in the zoo's new baboon exhibit. The protesters had gone, done leafleting the day's visitors. All the cars in the lot belonged to employees except a white van parked beside Paul's truck. He thought it belonged to the grad student who'd come to see Helena's research with Portia.

He checked his phone as he walked to his truck, and later he blamed that fact. There was a voice mail from Cameron, and he opened it as he reached the driver's door.

Someone beneath the truck grabbed his ankles. The van's passenger door opened, and a large man put a hood over his head. He shouted, swearing and dropping his phone as someone grabbed his wrist, but they tightened the hood, and there seemed to be three people forcing him into the back of the van.

He knew it must be the animal activists. He felt certain they wouldn't hurt him. But Cameron needed him. She was having bed rest, and she needed him to come home and make dinner, to run a bath for her.

He tried to talk, but the cloth was forced into his mouth.

His wrists were taped behind him with duct tape. They taped his legs together at his knees and ankles. The van started.

Who was going to make Cameron's dinner? Who was going to feed the dogs and Bertie?

"My fiancée's pregnant," he tried to say into the cloth. But it didn't even sound articulate to him.

WHERE WAS PAUL? It was unlike him to fail to answer the phone. Cameron had left him three voice mails and tried to keep herself from worrying with *Ina May's Guide to Breastfeeding,* which gave hopeful information on nursing preemies. She was at thirty-two weeks now, seemed enormous, and the baby, if born now, would soon be able to begin nursing.

Oh, where was Paul? Was he in a late meeting at the zoo? Surely he'd have called to tell her.

At seven-thirty, Cameron phoned Bridget and asked if she'd heard from her brother.

"No," Bridget said. "What's going on?"

Cameron told her about Paul's failure to come home. The sky was slowly growing dark.

"Do you have numbers for anyone else at the zoo?"

"Just the main number, and no one's answering."

"Look. The kids and I will drive out there and see if he's still there and get him to call you."

"Okay."

As Cameron hung up, she felt a slight cramp and wondered if she had to go to the bathroom. She got up and went into the bathroom.

Moments later, she saw that along with urine she'd left a mucous-like lump in the toilet. Her mucus plug. That must be what it was. She'd lost it.

Oh, hell.

Where was Paul?

Was this labor? Was she going into labor?

She hobbled back from the bathroom to the telephone.

PAUL AWOKE outside in the darkness and cold and saw stars overhead. His head ached, and he remembered being forced into the van. Now, he was lying on the forest floor, abandoned.

He sat up and found himself alone. Night. Where was he? No longer bound with duct tape. Free.

He stood slowly, feeling woozy, trying to think. He patted his pockets. No phone. Yes, he'd dropped it, hadn't he? Must have dropped the keys to the truck, too.

Keys.

Of course. He hadn't dropped the keys. They had wanted his keys and had undoubtedly gotten them. To release the animals.

His headache intensified, but he smiled. The protesters had foiled themselves. The new baboon exhibit and the chimp exhibit and the big cat house had been fitted with combination locks. No one but the keepers knew those numbers. Granted, the protesters could cause havoc in other areas. Briefly, he entertained happy visions of confrontations between protesters and, say, the hippopotamus—or the king cobra.

Really not funny. Bad for the animals, bad for the zoo.

He tried to orient. Was he still in the state park? He saw a hillside and walked in the opposite direction until he saw moonlight on asphalt. Yes, the road. He was still in the park and should go toward the zoo.

But what if they'd released the primates?

He had no phone. He saw a mile marker up ahead, then headlights illuminating the road, the headlights of a vehicle coming from the direction of the zoo.

Should he try to flag down the driver? He had no interest in again falling into the hands of the protesters.

He stepped back into the trees and saw the white van go by.

Had they gotten into the zoo? Had they released animals? Where was the nearest phone? Outside the ranger station, half a mile away.

He stepped back onto the shoulder and began walking.

"HIS TRUCK'S OUTSIDE the swimming pool, but he's not around." Bridget was talking on the phone from the back of her mother's car, stroking Cameron's hair as they drove to the hospital. She told the police, "Cameron says those animal protesters have been bothering him. Some people upset about the zoo taking the baboons? You know what I mean. I don't know *which* group. Does it matter?"

Cameron wondered what the protesters might have done to Paul, and then she couldn't think of it because another contraction came. She was only three centimeters dilated, but she'd never known such agony in her life. She cried out on a long moan.

This was a nightmare. Was there any way the baby could survive this? Something must be wrong for this to hurt so terribly.

They were in Clare's car because it would get them to the hospital faster than an ambulance. Clare had driven herself straight to Cameron's on hearing from her, and Bridget had met them there. Bridget had left her children with Sean, whom she'd called and asked for help. "Cameron's in labor?" he'd said. "Paul's missing?"

Bridget had growled, "Don't get your hopes up."

She'd told Cameron of this conversation, and Cameron thought of the fact that Paul was missing, that it made no sense for his truck to be at the swimming pool.

"The police are on it," Bridget said as she closed her phone. She held Cameron's wrist, checking her pulse. "How are you doing?"

Cameron was in terror of the next contraction. How did anyone withstand this? *Paul's not going to be here.* She wanted him to see their child born. She had wanted to *give birth,* not have the child cut out of her. Now she only wanted the pain to stop. How could she stand this pain, and the child was premature. Would the baby be all right? Could the baby survive what was happening?

The next contraction came with a pain that shrieked up her back.

"Try this." Bridget helped her onto hands and knees, steadied her in the moving vehicle.

Where was Paul? This was a nightmare. She'd been so foolish, so immature. She'd believed *he* wasn't ready for marriage. Even now she felt a stupid disappointment that there would be no homebirth, probably no natural birth, even no vaginal birth. Stupid for it to feel like failure. Soon her baby would be with her, hers and Paul's. Oh, God, if *only* the baby could make it. *Please hang in there, baby. Please be okay.*

The pain was a black hole, beyond all thought except *I can't do this. I will break apart. This is going to kill me.*

Bridget said, "You're doing great, Cameron. You're doing so well."

"Hospital," Cameron choked, feeling so terrified, for the baby's life, for her own. This couldn't be normal pain. This was anguish. This was hell, the hell in which she'd seen Beatrice but surely worse. No one could control this, no one could stop it.

"We're almost there. Here, we're at the door."

Cameron got out of the car under her own steam and was guided into a wheelchair. *I don't want to sit down. I can't.* She bent forward with her head between her knees and vomited, and at the same moment there was an enormous gushing between her legs, water breaking, and more screaming pain.

"Good." Bridget's voice was at her ear, Clare walking fast beside them.

But it was Bridget Cameron wanted, clinging to Paul's sister's hand. "Where's Paul?"

"I don't know. We're finding him, honey. Don't worry."

A POLICE CRUISER picked Paul up just outside the ranger station. They had been notified by his sister, they said, that he hadn't returned from work. One of the officers was a man who had responded to the incident at the Women's Resource Center, with the belligerent ex-partner named Jerry, and he asked after Cameron.

Paul needed to call her, and he asked to use a cell phone, his own being missing. One of the officers let Paul use his phone, and Paul called Cameron's house, then her cell phone. His first call was picked up by the answering machine; the next call connected him to her voice mail. In the zoo parking lot, he found his cell phone, but it had been run over, undoubtedly intentionally, undoubtedly by the activists.

He tried his mother's house, to see if she had heard from Cameron because he was feeling uneasy about his fiancée. She would have been worried when he hadn't come home. But his mother didn't answer, either. He would try her cell phone after he discovered what was happening inside the zoo.

The activists had succeeded in creating considerable havoc, despite being foiled by the new combination locks. Not all animals had been so protected. As Paul had predicted, the Reptile House had suffered, the backs of several snake exhibits opened and their inhabitants gone. As a former reptile keeper, Paul knew he could be of use in hunting down the escapees, but his mind was still on the fact that he hadn't gotten hold of Cameron.

The wolves had been freed, as well, but they had not gone. They were creatures of habit, used to their home at the zoo, reluctant to venture into the keeper area, shy of people. Two grizzly bears had torn apart their keeper area, opening the refrigerator and helping themselves to its contents, ransacking the garbage. They had to be darted to be moved out of the keeper area.

The king cobra was simply gone, presenting a puzzle, and while Paul shined a flashlight all about the area outside the Reptile House, puzzling over where the sixteen-foot venomous snake might have gone, he used the veterinarian's phone to try to reach his mother.

"Paul?" she said when she answered, probably second sight kicking in to tell her that it was actually her son on the phone. "Cameron's in labor."

"Where is she?"

"We're at the hospital."

"I'll be right there." A colleague had moved his truck back from the pool to outside the zoo. The protesters had left the keys.

After speaking to the veterinarian and returning the phone, he met the zoo director entering the zoo.

"Where are you going?" Dr. Bannister demanded.

"My girl—fiancée—is in labor."

The director looked shocked that Paul should have impregnated an unmarried woman. Dr. Bannister was the kind of person to be shocked by such a thing. In fact, he'd once expressed concern to Paul about children who were visiting the zoo possibly witnessing primates mating.

"Where are the apes?" he demanded, apparently recovering from hearing of human reproductive behavior unsanctioned by matrimony.

"All accounted for," Paul answered. As were the other primate exhibits.

"Reptiles?"

"You'll see." It was a bad time to have to leave, but he needed to be with Cameron in her labor, to be with her as their child was born. She must not have to go through labor without him. He could think of nothing else.

"You can't leave!" the director told him. "We need you. Are there animals out?"

Paul pretended he was in too much of a hurry to hear.

CAMERON SAW HIM when he entered her room, but his presence no longer seemed a matter of urgency to her. She was delirious with pain, plain old pain. All the romantic words she'd heard, contractions described as "rushes," seemed unfair tricks. A nurse had checked her two minutes before, said, "She's not dilating," as though Cameron couldn't hear her.

Cameron knew that failure to progress right now would mean a cesarean. Her water had broken. But she was on her back, in agony, and the nurse suggested an epidural.

Cameron shook her head.

"It might let you stay with it," the nurse said.

Cameron looked into Bridget's eyes.

Bridget said, "Whatever you want."

Two nurses came in and looked at the screen for the electronic fetal monitor.

Paul crouched down beside the bed. He said nothing, just gazed at her steadily, bringing a quiet that Cameron wanted.

Then it happened.

Fetal distress.

And she was wheeled toward the O.R., Paul coming along, being given a mask, a hat to cover his hair. And there she was given an epidural, and as the pain eased she thought only of the baby, that she would see the baby soon. *And please let the baby be all right.*

Paul watched the obstetrician make an incision, watched his child born by cesarean section. It was a girl, and when he saw her he thought that she seemed to have come from some alien, holy place. Her face scrunched up, she breathed, and Dr. Henderson showed her to Cameron before she was taken away to the NICU.

Cameron said, "Gabriela?"

Paul nodded, gazing down at her face, overwhelmed by her courage. "I like it."

"Go with her," Cameron said. "Go ahead. Don't wait here."

Paul wanted to stay with Cameron while the surgeon sewed her up, but he understood her desire that they shouldn't both be so long separated from the baby.

IN A SHORT TIME, they wheeled Cameron down into the NICU so that she could look at Gabriela in her incubator. The premature newborn had tubes in her nose, forcing oxygen in, yet she was extremely beautiful. Cameron had wanted so badly to be able to give birth vaginally, but now it didn't matter. Little Gabriela was alive and, though premature, her lungs not yet fully developed, she was healthy.

They held her the next day, sitting back in a reclining chair made for the purpose, Cameron first allowed to hold the tiny child against her bare skin, her warmth helping to keep Gabriela warm. Paul was next.

In the coming days, Cameron learned to pump breast milk, which was scanty at first. Paul took to softly singing lullabies to Gabriela during his turns holding her in the NICU. They were both constantly at the hospital, where all Cameron's family, including Nanna, came to see her and Gabriela. Though all the milk Gabriela received was pumped from Cameron, the baby would not be allowed to go home until she could breastfeed.

Sean came once to see the baby and Cameron. The birth of Gabriela seemed to signal to him that Cameron was truly unavailable, and her text messages from him ceased. Part of her wondered—irrationally, she knew— if she seemed defective to him for having given birth to a premature baby by cesarean section. She knew Paul did not perceive her that way. Yet she almost perceived herself that way. It didn't matter, of course. Gabriela was healthy, and that was what mattered.

Together, Cameron and Paul shared the daily milestones. Cameron was in love with her baby, glad when more milk began coming in, thankful to be able to pump breast milk for Gabriela. Then, after a week, Gabriela was deemed strong enough to begin nursing, and that was another new and wonderful sensation.

Cameron and Paul spent as much time as possible

holding their daughter, Paul coming by every lunchtime from the zoo, despite the distance. The hospital was always his first stop after work.

When Cameron was able to go home from the hospital, instead of returning immediately to work, she continued to go to the hospital each day to spend as much time as possible with Gabriela.

Cameron felt more committed than ever to Paul since Gabriela's birth, and she tried to stave off any insecurity caused by knowing he'd been given a love potion. Rather, she tried to look forward to planning their wedding.

But Paul did not mention the wedding. Gabriela's birth certificate read Gabriela McAllister Cureux, but Cameron knew this was not synonymous with herself and Paul being married. Had he developed "cold feet," and where had that expression come from anyhow?

She wanted to sound him out and wasn't sure how. One night, three weeks after Gabriela's birth, when they returned late from the hospital, she said casually, "You know it would probably be nice for her if we got married."

Paul, driving his truck, said, "I don't want to do that until she comes home. I want her to be there."

Cameron assessed the answer for sincerity. It wasn't an unreasonable wish, although it certainly wasn't the usual thing for a newborn to attend her parents' wedding. She didn't fault Paul for an unconventional wish—as long as it didn't hide another motive. As long as it didn't hide his not wanting to marry her at all.

Granted, Paul had been busy with things other than

their new daughter. There had been long sessions with the police regarding the protesters' kidnapping him. The zoo had been closed for several days while employees searched for the king cobra. They found him at last, trapped in a pipe that was too small for him. He had died in his struggles to free himself. The zoo had been featured in news articles all over the state because of the mischief caused by the protesters. Paul had had a "relationship" with the cobra when he was a reptile keeper, and the snake's death had saddened and angered him.

As they reached Cameron's house, she asked him how that day had gone at the zoo.

He sighed, not wanting to talk about the sakis. The male appeared not to like his mate, and the mate—to Paul—appeared injured by the fact. Her mothering was haphazard at best, though the baby wasn't starving or anything. "Everything's fine," he said.

Cameron thought of her own job, which she loved. When Gabriela came home, Cameron would be able to go back to work and take the baby with her.

The dogs greeted them outside. Inside, Bertie stepped out of the bedroom to look at them, then went to the kitchen.

Paul said, "So…you seem pretty healed up."

Warmth rushed through her at his words. They had not had intercourse for months and hadn't done any kind of lovemaking since Gabriela's birth.

"I'm healed," she answered, smiling when he looked at her.

"Meet you in the bedroom."

IT FELT LIKE A CENTURY since they'd made love. The love-making was interrupted by episodes of her milk leaking, but they laughed, too, and were both glad to have intimacy restored.

The day Gabriela came home, Bridget and her children, as well as Cameron's mother, were on hand to welcome the baby. Cameron relaxed in the pleasure of nursing her daughter at the kitchen table. Paul was at the zoo. When Bridget and her children left, Cameron's mother remained.

"Now you and Paul *are* planning to marry, aren't you?" she said.

It was inevitable, Cameron supposed. The Billingham genes decreed that people who weren't married did not live together, let alone raise a child together.

"We're engaged," Cameron said simply. "We've both been focused on Gabriela, Mom. And nothing's going to change once we are married." Cameron was certain of this. "We're married now, for all intents and purposes."

Her mother knew when she was beaten—or rather when she couldn't get what she wanted immediately. But Cameron knew the subject would come up again.

When Paul came home from the zoo, she mentioned her mother's remark.

"We may as well do it," he said with a shrug. "When do you think?"

Cameron had hoped for more enthusiasm. At least, he hadn't again suggested putting off setting a date. Well, she shouldn't quibble with it. They got along, were best friends, and if the love potion was wearing off, that was all to the good. She hated artifice. Even if they were both marrying simply for Gabriela, that was all right.

Yet she couldn't escape a slight depression at the thought that Paul spoke of their wedding with so little interest.

"Why do people get married?" she asked as she scooped up Bertie the cat, posing the question to the animal.

"All kinds of reasons," Paul answered, stepping into the bedroom to gaze at their daughter.

"Bridget," Cameron told him, still speaking from the kitchen, "says people marry for first chakra reasons: survival."

"That sounds like Bridget," he murmured.

"Obviously, some people fall in love and get married," she remarked, following him into the bedroom to see Gabriela, too. "Then, everything happens in the right order. Engagement, marriage, children."

Paul stared at her. He said, "I would never have suspected you of being *wedded*," he used the word intentionally, "to such a traditional timeline."

"Obviously, I'm not," she snapped.

"I think you are. Being that you became pregnant before marriage, I should have promptly proposed and married you, before your pregnancy test had a chance to dry."

"That's *not* true, and *nothing* about Gabriela is unfortunate."

"I'm glad we agree on that." He sat down on the edge of the bed, feet from where the infant was sleeping. "You keep getting upset about this wedding thing. What's the problem?"

She let Bertie down to the ground and used her fingers to enumerate. "One, you didn't want to marry me at all until you drank Bridget's love potion. Two, now you're marrying me so that Gabriela's parents will be married."

"I'm *what?*"

"At your core, you're more conventional than I am. You're not in love with me. You don't even care about sex with me particularly."

Paul stared at her, wondering if she'd gone mad. "I *am* in love with you. You just gave birth to my child!"

"See! That's not being in love with me; it's being in love with yourself. She's *our* child anyhow."

"And what's this about my indifference to sex?"

"I didn't say you were indifferent."

"Is this more about your wanting me to show emotion? Cameron, I've done everything I can to convince you that I love you. Maybe the doubt is in yourself. Is there a chance you don't feel worthy of being loved?"

Cameron listened to his words and was further angered by them and knew her anger to be somewhat irrational. His saying that he knew no other way to convince her of his love seemed true. She didn't know what would convince her—except his being so. Which she believed he wasn't.

"Also," he added, "what you've said makes no sense. Either I drank the love potion and am in love with you only because of it or I'm not in love with you and am marrying you only because of Gabriela. I can't win. Are you telling me that *you* don't want to be married?"

She did want to be married, and she felt foolish for

practically begging for proof of his love. He had *told* her he loved her. What more should she expect?

"No," she said. "I want to marry you."

Paul hesitated only a moment before replying, "Good."

"*That* sounded enthusiastic."

"We've been fighting, and we're not even married yet. How do you expect me to sound enthusiastic?"

"Is marriage a lifetime commitment for you?" she asked, suspicious.

"Oh, yes," he replied emphatically, and she knew he was thinking of the disruption caused by divorce in his own childhood.

She decided to drop the subject, to let *him* bring up the idea of setting a date. She wondered how many years she'd have to wait.

CHAPTER THIRTEEN

PAUL WAS GLAD that Cameron seemed to drop her agitation about marriage. He was loath to propose that she name the date for fear of hearing more stupid accusations of his lack of love for her. What he wanted to see happened. Peace. Cameron took Gabriela to work with her on every day but his weekday off, when he liked to care for the baby. At night, when he got home, he found his child and his best friend, his beloved, who seemed to be recovering much of her spirit.

He loved playing his guitar for Cameron and Gabriela, and the only gigs he accepted were for a daytime birthday party and a concert in the park. His father asked him one day, "So when are you two actually going to get married?"

Paul said simply, "I don't know." But when he returned from the zoo one day in early October, he asked Cameron, "So...shall we set a date?" He hardly knew how to sound as he asked, and he told himself that it was because she'd been so damned desperate for marriage. Cameron! Who had pretended to be his girlfriend for years, who had been, he'd thought, as wary of commitment as himself.

Cameron, who was carrying Gabriela in a sling against her chest as she cut vegetables for dinner, kept her own voice level. "Sure. How is November for you?"

"Is that too soon?" he asked.

Cameron considered. Yes, weddings did take time to plan. Yet she heard no enthusiasm in Paul's voice and could awaken no answering enthusiasm in herself because of *his* lack of enthusiasm. Somehow, the dream of being married to him had become tarnished in her mind.

"Let's just go to the courthouse some day," she said. "I don't need a big wedding." As she spoke, she was conscious that wanting her to have a real wedding was the reason Paul had given for postponing the wedding till after Gabriela's birth. She looked down at her baby daughter's precious head, with its tufts of dark hair. *You're the one I'm in love with,* she thought, comforted. She added, "I don't want a big wedding."

And it was true. The wedding no longer mattered. Paul and she both felt that their being married would be best for Gabriela. This was what she told herself and tried to believe, that the two of them felt the same. But as she spoke, she realized that it wasn't how she felt.

That she didn't want to be married to him at all, not on such apathetic terms.

She said, "Let's just skip it."

"What?" He had crouched down to pet Mariah.

"Why get married? We're fine as we are," she said. "As a matter of fact, there's no reason for you to live here now."

Paul said, "I *want* to live here. You're my family."

Cameron was satisfied by the answer, felt comfort in it. "Well, being married won't make that any more true."

Paul felt as though he'd taken a wrong step somewhere, and he could not go back and retrace it no matter how hard he tried. He knew what the wrong step was. It was that he hadn't immediately asked Cameron to marry him within five minutes of learning she was pregnant. Never mind that Cameron's point of view was entirely unreasonable, never mind that she never came out and said that was the problem. He knew it was, and her attitude annoyed him.

Now she didn't want to get married?

He said, "We're engaged. Doesn't that mean that next thing we get married?" He tried to put some humor in his voice and feared he sounded cynical instead.

"There's no need." She looked down at the ring on her hand, put down the knife, slid the ring off, turned and tried to put it in his hand. "Really. Let's just say we're as committed now as we'll ever be."

He stood but didn't take the ring. He didn't know what to do. "Are you breaking our engagement? Are you saying you don't want to marry me?"

"Not especially," Cameron answered, rubbing Gabriela's tiny back through the cloth of the sling. She tried to put the ring in his hand.

"I don't want to give that to anyone else," he said.

Her cheeks pinked slightly, and a small smile formed on her lips. "Okay." She started to put it back on, but Gabriela shifted then and made a soft cry.

Paul slid the ring onto Cameron's finger.

She grinned. "Thank you."

He bit his lip, not sure what to say or do. He went to the sink to wash his hands. Cameron sat down at the table to nurse Gabriela. Almost automatically, Paul filled a quart juice jar with water and set it in front of her on the table. Nursing required her to drink an incredible amount of water.

"Thank you," she murmured.

He touched her hair before returning to his work at the counter. His back to her, Paul asked, "Have you ever considered what I said to you before, that maybe you don't feel worthy of being loved?"

"I feel worthy." Cameron gazed into Gabriela's dark eyes, which watched her. They were the shape of Paul's, Cameron thought, and Cameron believed she might have a Cureux nose. The milk flowed from her breasts, tingling, warm, and she was joyful and content in oneness with her child. She admired Gabriela's miniature fingernails. She loved everything about the little girl and thought her the most beautiful baby she had ever seen.

Paul turned from the sink to look at the two of them. He loved them both so much. He said, "Cameron, I *want* to marry you. I want you for my wife."

She looked up and saw the steadiness of his gaze. He did sound sincere. *What's my problem?* she thought. She had wanted to marry him, but she'd wanted all of him and hadn't quite believed all of him was committed to her. And now he was watching her nurse their child, so of course he leaned toward commitment, perhaps even yearned for it. She said, "Thank you for saying so."

"I'm not *saying* it. I *mean* it."

"I know. Thank you. Let's not worry about it right now. I have your grandmother's ring, and we're a family, and let's leave things that way."

Paul swallowed and turned back to the sink. Well. It was the kind of arrangement he'd have found just about perfect at one point. He still found it that way except for a single thing.

He kept thinking of the sakis, of the male ignoring his mate, of her inner collapse.

He'd done Cameron some deep injury by not immediately wishing to marry her. He felt he'd hurt her in a way that had formed a scar, and the scar was what lay between them, and he didn't know how to heal it.

Yes, he'd spent most of their acquaintance feeling that he *never* wanted to make a lifetime commitment to any woman. He'd been unable to imagine submitting himself to the constraints of wife and family.

But caring for Cameron during her pregnancy, seeing Gabriela born and Cameron's struggles with sore nipples, her devotion to their child had changed him so deeply that he felt unlike the person he'd been before. He'd begun to think of life insurance policies. Cameron's medical insurance was covered through her work as his was through the zoo. But he was thinking, talking to her, of enlarging her house, making another bedroom for Gabriela when she was older. Now the baby slept with them.

Why did Cameron not want to marry him?

Silly reasons. Constantly doubting his love, his devotion to her and their child.

He tried to put it all out of his mind as he stir-fried vegetables and chicken, as he checked the soup simmering on the stove.

THERE WAS NO ONE to whom Paul could speak of what was going on between Cameron and himself. No one but her, and those conversations had become less and less productive.

And at the zoo on the following day, when the male saki finally showed some interest in his mate, she yelled at him in the saki language, made faces and pelted him with anything at hand, except their infant.

Watching, Paul covered his own face. There was nothing he could do about this situation any more than he could correct his own. The junior keeper, a woman, who witnessed with him the female's response, said, "He should have been nicer earlier. She doesn't like him anymore."

Great, Paul thought, considering his own situation. *Just great.*

Because he *had* been "nice."

In the wild, the male perhaps would have won his position with his mate by securing resources for her, special things. Paul remembered all he'd tried to do for Cameron during her bed rest. He thought he had done everything in his power to show his love for her. But she had turned that into devotion for their baby.

Now she seemed uncertain that he wanted to marry her simply because he loved her and wanted to be her husband and wanted her to be his wife. It occurred to him to snatch her and Gabriela away to an elopement. To do something extremely romantic. Yet he was having a hard time finding the inspiration, and where could he take her that would be romantic? How could he create the romance she seemed to need so much?

THAT AFTERNOON at the Women's Resource Center, just as Cameron had finished nursing Gabriela in her office, she heard the bell signaling the opening of the front door. She settled the sleeping infant in her bassinet, then opened the door of her office and stepped out. The newcomer, a pretty woman, was crying hysterically. While her two puzzled children played with toys in the lobby, Cameron took her back to her own office. Calming the woman, who said her name was Tammy, Cameron listened and tried to understand her story.

"I don't know if this is the place to come. I don't know if there is anywhere to come."

Cameron was not a psychotherapist, and though she was often the first person to hear clients' stories, she generally listened, then let the women know what would be available through the Women's Resource Center, called someone to take the families to the safe house if necessary, tried to make the clients feel welcome.

"He never wanted to marry me." He, Cameron had gathered, was the father of the two-year-old, the younger child in the next room. The mother was still sobbing. "He never married me, and now he has someone else. It's not right. He had a child with me. He should marry me."

Cameron tried to be blank as a slate, even within herself,

yet the subject at hand seemed close to her own. But Paul *was* willing to marry her; she was the one pushing him away because he hadn't immediately wanted marriage.

"He's mine," the woman continued, against evidence to the contrary, the father of her child living with another woman.

This was something a counselor could explain to the client. Cameron said, "Let me explain about the services we offer here. You may want to avail yourself of counseling services. If you haven't been able to collect child support, we'll connect you with social services. They're the experts at that, and they'll make sure he pays."

"I don't want child support. I want him!"

Cameron stared at the woman. She *was* very pretty, with well-defined cheekbones and long, straight dark hair, but Cameron was amazed that even a beautiful woman should have lived to the age of twenty-six without realizing there were some things she might never get and that other people could not be controlled.

Uneasily, she thought again of Paul, of *her* refusal to marry him. The woman before her sounded childish, and Cameron felt that she'd been childish. No, she was certain of it.

It took an hour and a half to calm the woman down, get her an appointment with a counselor and finally get her out the door.

By the time she left, it was almost five, and Cameron was glad to put Gabriela in the car and drive both of them home. Her mind rebelled against the discovery of the afternoon. Well, not discovery. But suddenly she could see herself clearly, see how unreasonable she'd been.

Gabriela awoke when they got home, and as Cameron nursed her, she again considered the question Paul had twice asked her. Did she feel worthy of being loved?

She did. That was a solution that sounded brilliant and simply wasn't. The fact was, her pride had been hurt by his not immediately deciding he wanted to marry her. Her pride was further hurt when it appeared to her that he would never have asked her to marry him at all if Bridget hadn't given him a love potion.

How could she make up to him for the way she had acted? When she thought of all he had done for her during her pregnancy, she felt an appalling sense of having done absolutely everything wrong.

When Gabriela fell asleep, Cameron got up and began preparing dinner. She took a moment out from cooking to go outside and collect some fall leaves, then arrange them on a plate inside to enjoy their colors. What would Paul most want that she could give him?

Possibly simply the acknowledgment that she believed in his love, and she felt as much at a loss to show that as he must have all these long months of her rejection. Because that was what it had been. She had continually told him that what he was doing was not enough.

She listened for his truck and felt herself draw a breath of relief when she heard it outside the house.

She went to the door and found him bringing in paper bags containing wood of various sizes. She had a sun-room on the porch and he used that for what woodworking he'd done since they'd lived together. It was now home to a table saw and quite a few other tools.

She kissed him and said, "I have to tell you something."

His glance was interested. "Let me put this stuff in the sunroom. It's a not-very-practical project, but I'm going to try my hand at it."

"What is it?"

"You'll see. Or it will be a disaster and you won't see because no one will be able to figure it out."

Cameron followed him into the sunroom and sat down on one of the chairs.

He said, "I brought us a movie, too." He pulled out *Wuthering Heights* with Laurence Olivier and Merle Oberon.

"Hooray," said Cameron. "Of course, Mary Anne maintains that Heathcliff is much too toned down in the movie, but I like it."

"Is it very different from the book?"

"Have you ever read the book?"

He shook his head.

"He's not the sort of person anyone should want to marry except the woman who didn't marry him, because she was the only person he loved." She drew her eyebrows together a bit, puzzling over it. "He's really a bit like the guys we see at the Women's Resource Center, but there's something different there. I can't put my finger on it."

Abruptly, she changed the subject. "Paul, I've been a jerk to you. I've been childish, really horrible."

Paul's first thought was that she was going to tell him to move out, that she was actually looking for something different in a man.

She said, "Can we get married at the zoo?"

Paul laughed. The zoo could be hired out for private parties, and undoubtedly this was what Cameron had in mind. "Of course."

"I want to get married in front of the wolves."

"I know some other animals that could really benefit from the example," he couldn't help saying. Quickly, he added, "But your wish is my command."

"You mean the sakis?" she asked sympathetically. "Aren't things any better?"

"No. But we'll get married wherever you like." He sat down in the chair nearest hers and scooted it closer. "Cameron, I'm sorry I was so anti-commitment. You've got to understand— My parents. It was pretty crazy. Not their divorce. But my mother is a formidable woman with very exact ideas. I loved being alone, being free, a bachelor, without having to consider anyone else's wants or needs. It's easy to say I was immature, but it's not that simple. I was—and am, to some degree—selfish. I thought being married would be too difficult for me. But living with you is easy. You're like part of myself. I don't ever want to live without you."

Cameron clung tightly to his hand, hearing the words she'd so long yearned to hear, convincing her that he was truly committed to her.

"I was immature," she said. "Not realistic."

He shook his head. "Romantic. And I like that about

you. I've never been in love before, Cameron. With anyone."

He saw the smile in her brown eyes.

"But are you going to give me time to finish my project before the wedding?" he asked.

GABRIELA WAS TEETHING, and Paul, seeing Cameron exhausted from nursing, took the baby out to the living room. He scouted Cameron's bookshelves until he found a battered copy of *Wuthering Heights,* not the vintage edition Sean had given her but a paperback that appeared to have been read and reread. He took a teething ring from the freezer where it had been cooling for Gabriela and settled on the couch with the book and the still hiccupping infant.

Wolfie had come inside, and during Gabriela's recent crying the animal had inched closer and closer to her and Paul. Paul, the most detached of animal lovers, couldn't help thinking that the shy animal wanted to comfort the baby.

He read *Wuthering Heights* for two hours and dozed off with Gabriela asleep on his chest. Later, he was not sure what awoke him. But two wolfish eyes were right beside him with Wolfie's partly gray muzzle. The wild dog's tongue touched Gabriela's face, but when he saw Paul's eyes—now open—he backed up and edged back to lie down near the doorway.

Paul smiled. Cradling the baby against him, he got up of the couch to switch off the living room light and go into the bedroom where Cameron slept.

PAUL AND CAMERON decided to marry during the week after Christmas, when Paul was sure his project would be done. Cameron eschewed a wedding dress and bought some new pants and a flowing blouse and covered both with her hooded camel's hair coat. Because of the likelihood of snow—and so that her grandmother could attend the ceremony—Cameron decided the best spot for the wedding would be the interior of the winter saki exhibit.

The veterinarian, amused, later said that during the ceremony the female had let the male within five feet of her, which was progress.

After the ceremony, everyone had refreshments in the warmth of the Reptile House, a quieter setting than among the primates, and Cameron's grandmother remarked, "Well, I've never been to a wedding like this."

Cameron stood beside Paul and watched Bridget's children chase Sean Devlin through the building. She told him, "*I'm* not the kind of person to give anyone a love potion."

Paul said, "And *he* doesn't deserve it."

He and Cameron gazed over at Bridget, her short dark hair in a boyish bob, long bangs curling back from her strong face, who was talking to Mary Anne about Mary Anne's pregnancy. He shook his head. "I would *never* do that to anyone."

"Very honorable," Cameron agreed.

Paul's father appeared with Gabriela in his arms.

"She's looking hungry and starting to get a little cranky," he told Cameron, handing her the baby. Cameron and Paul went to sit in chairs near the monitor lizards. When Paul stood up, Clare Cureux took his seat.

Cameron remembered the confession Clare had made to her son months before, the thing she had done to preserve her career as a midwife. Like Paul, she somewhat doubted that the sacrifice had been necessary. Surely, no court would have convicted Clare of anything.

It wasn't something Cameron could ever mention to her, imagining the shame Clare must still carry over the incident.

Clare smiled at mother and daughter as Cameron nursed Gabriela. "Bridget looked like that," she remarked. "That nose. I'll have to show you baby pictures."

Cameron was grateful for this, for this simple warmth, comparatively rare in her interactions with Paul's mother.

Clare said, "Well, I have a present for you and Paul, out in the car. It's not wrapped, so I'll tell you what it is. My mother's wedding ring quilt."

"Thank you!" Cameron exclaimed, knowing the quilt. "Are you sure?"

"Oh, yes. I have other quilts of hers, and I gave Bridget one on her marriage." A look of sadness crossed Clare's face, sadness and concern for Bridget's widowed state, Cameron supposed.

Cameron said, "Clare, I know you don't—well, approve—of love potions. Yet you make them."

"*Approve* isn't the right word." Clare frowned as she formulated her thoughts. "I make them because they are part of my family heritage—and not a part I find disgraceful. My mother made them and her mother before that. It is a family recipe, if you will, and each of us has slightly altered ingredients, because the ingredients aren't the essential elements."

"It's your gift," Cameron articulated.

"Well—" Clare was obviously uncomfortable discussing it.

"Have you ever refused one to someone?"

Clare didn't have to think. "No."

Cameron looked at her. "But surely some people want to, say, steal someone else's spouse." Or *fiancé,* she thought, remembering details of Mary Anne's buying a love potion.

"These potions have a way of taking care of themselves. The person who buys the potion…" Clare gave a smile that, to Cameron, seemed sad. "There's always a need for more love in the world, Cameron, and the people who buy these potions need love. And love changes them, changes everyone, for the better."

Cameron couldn't argue with that. "Have you ever given a love potion to someone? I mean, administered it?"

"Never."

There was an absolute finality to the word. Cameron considered Bridget, who seemed to brew and distribute love potions with a slightly cavalier attitude. "Have you ever been afraid that, say, Bridget, might give you one?"

Clare laughed. "Why on Earth would she?"

"When you divorced—" Cameron wished she hadn't asked the question.

"Bridget was a little girl. What she knew in life was her parents living apart."

And Paul, a little older, who remembered something

different, didn't have the Cureux gift for making the draughts—or the desire to give them to anyone.

Cameron bit her lip and thought of all the women who had come to the Women's Resource Center, all the stories she'd heard. *Paul shouldn't have told me,* she thought. About what his mother had done. But Cameron supposed he'd had to tell someone.

Clare said, "So Paul told you."

Cameron had forgotten, forgotten the Cureux Sight. Clare must have sensed.

She grasped Clare's strong brown hand with its prominent veins, realizing as she did that it was the first time she had held Clare's hand, though Bridget's had been constantly in hers during labor. "If you ever need to talk about it, there are counselors at the resource center—or I can find you someone out of town."

Clare shook her head. "It happened a long time ago. And I chose it, Cameron. I was very young. My clients were the most important thing to me, and I did what I thought was best for them. Today, things are different. And perhaps I should have fought it back then. Midwives spend so much time in court, defending themselves, fighting for the right to practice. They all simply want to care for their clients, but they also feel a need to stand up for all midwives, to change the laws, to draw more women to homebirth and to midwifery-based care. I felt that life was too short—and those few women in my care, too important. It was disgraceful, but it was a choice I made."

Cameron nodded, puzzling over the dilemma. "Would you do the same thing today?"

Clare shrugged. "Today, I'd accept the fine and the brief jail time for practicing without a license. Of course, they might try to make it manslaughter. And they could have then. The people were gone, only their stillborn child left as evidence. Probably, it would have meant a long time in court, and if I'd practiced during that time..."

Cameron considered all of it and believed that she, if she'd been Clare, would have taken the other road. Her family would have come first. Not to mention trading her body for...

After leaving Clare, Cameron sat next to her grandmother for a half hour and heard Jacqueline Billingham describe her own wedding and honeymoon in Charleston. Cameron and Paul had not planned a honeymoon yet. It seemed strange to them to bring one's baby daughter on a honeymoon and neither wanted to be parted from her while she was still so young, so Paul was planning something for the future.

That night, when the three of them went home, Cameron felt a deep contentment. She and Paul were married, and their wedding had been exactly as she would have wished it.

When they had settled Gabriela, Cameron said, "I want to give you your wedding present."

"Likewise," he said, grinning, because the secretive project in the sunroom seemed to have taken on a life of its own. Two weeks before, he'd taken to throwing a sheet over it when he wasn't working on it. Cameron was pretty sure it was a dollhouse. She'd never had one, had always been a tomboy, but she liked the idea of having a dollhouse.

She went into the bedroom and returned with a package she'd wrapped the week before. She hadn't had the slightest idea what to give him for a wedding gift, spending much time pondering the things that were most important to him and trying to find something that would be both useful and special.

What she'd done had taken time. Paul said, "Should I open it now?"

"Yes."

"Let's take it in the sunroom."

And in the sunroom, the dollhouse stood unveiled. Cameron gazed at it in initial wonder, then came closer to study it, turning on two lamps to see better as Paul unwrapped her present to him.

It was a photograph album, containing photos she'd collected from both their lives and from their life together. She'd added, beneath some of the photos, poems and quotes from favorite books and aphorisms and paradoxes she'd read and liked. Paul grinned as he turned pages, laughed at an Oscar Wilde quote, gazed in rapture at a photo of Cameron holding Gabriela in the NICU.

Cameron could hardly spare attention for his reaction to her gift. Her heart soared as she saw what Paul had assembled, what he'd created for her.

Someone—a local artist, she discovered by the signature—had painted on canvas a backdrop that stretched behind the dollhouse, windy moors with rocky outcroppings and wild birds in flight. But the house. Outside the structure, slanted firs and gaunt thorns stood as though blown by the wind. Miniscule threads of grass grew up

between tiny flagstones leading to the door. Even miniature griffins were there, weathered and crumbling over
the door. The windows were narrow, the corners enforced
with round pebbles, like river stones. And at the garret
window of the rambling wooden house were two
amazing dolls, dark-haired and dark-eyed, tiny and
perfect. And there were others too, other dolls, other
characters, other times, and over the door was a wooden
sign dated with the year 1500 reading HARETON
EARNSHAW, and the dark interior had a great fireplace
with an assortment of guns over it. It was a place she had
read described but seen only in her mind's eye. Tears
sprang into her eyes. "I love it so much." He had made
her Wuthering Heights.

Her reaction was everything Paul wanted, the tangible
sign of the complete redemption he'd wanted for months,
her letting go of what he'd been unable to be in the past
and accepting and loving utterly what he was now.

He laid aside his own gift from her to enjoy later while
he showed her all the dolls that Mary Anne had helped
him find and remake into Cathy and Heathcliff as
children and teenagers and adults, of old Mr. Earnshaw
and Hindley Earnshaw and Edgar and Isabella Linton and
old Nellie Dean and Joseph and Catherine Linton Heathcliff and Hareton and Linton Heathcliff, and all the dogs
and even the tenant Mr. Lockwood, to whom Nellie Dean
told the story.

And Cameron spotted, in the clouds and wind across
the moors, two ghostly figures leaving footprints, just im-
pressions of the nature around them, but hand in hand.

She and Paul stayed up for hours thinking of ways to recreate the books Mr. Lockwood found on his first night at Wuthering Heights, discussing ideas for more furniture, plans for the stable, and Paul's hunt for Heathcliff's and Hareton's dogs.

Cameron whispered, "I never had a dollhouse before. And this is so much more than a dollhouse. This is a world come alive."

When she could finally bring herself to leave it and come to bed, she and Paul lay down with Gabriela between them, and she reached over the baby to touch her husband's face. "I'm so happy."

"We both are," he told her. They breathed in the dark while snow fell outside the windows. "Do you remember that night at school? Halloween?"

Cameron laughed. "Of course, I do."

"I had glitter in my bed." He laughed. "Maybe that's how I knew you were the one."

"You *didn't* know," she answered. "You told me it would get in the way of our friendship, or something like that."

"Cameron, I knew that you—whatever I had with you—was something I didn't want to destroy. And back then I probably would have destroyed it."

"Oh, right," she said, disbelieving.

"You were my best friend. Still are."

They put their heads together on the pillow to kiss.

"I don't think I'm going to be able to sleep," she said. "I'm too happy."

Paul touched her hair.

She asked, "Do you think Bridget…and Sean…?"

Paul propped himself up on his arm to shake his head at her. "Don't even think about it."

"I can *think* about it. And your mother says she's never refused anyone a love potion."

Suddenly Mariah sat up from where she lay on her bed. She lifted her head. Outside, her father howled and Mariah joined in, singing with him.

Cameron teased Paul. "It's a sign. A sign that I should…"

Paul carefully climbed over Gabriela and around to the other side of his wife. "A sign that I need to help you get sleepy."

With his body against hers she knew a perfect completeness. She was home. He was home to her—Paul, with Gabriela there close to them. And she understood the unreachable maleness of him yet how their souls were alike. She whispered, "'Whatever souls are made of, his and mine are the same.'"

Paul said, "When I read those words, I could only think of you and me."

She held him more tightly and knew she had never been happier and that each day to come she could be more so. And she could bring ever deeper happiness to this man she so loved.

She said, "Oh, thank you, thank you," and she was speaking not just to him but to the divine that had made her love with him possible, to the gifts of this full moon of life.

His cheek was against hers, and she thought there was dampness there between them, and she looked at him in the dark and touched his eyelashes and tried, for him and who he was, the man he was, to not show she noticed their wetness. And he behaved as though it wasn't happening and kissed her mouth. She wanted no more.

IN THE DARKNESS of the primate exhibit, the male saki, who should have been asleep, saw his chance. He picked up the soft red thing and carried it back up into trees where he preferred to be. His mate ignored him, was probably sleeping, the baby nestled against her.

He did not know that the soft thing he'd taken from the floor was supposed to be a fire truck, just knew that sometimes, if you hit the soft things, something happened.

He banged the fire truck on a tree branch, and a wailing sound cried through the exhibit. He hit it against the tree branch again. When the wailing died, he struck it a third time and listened to the strange cry rise and fall. In the silence, he prepared to hit it again.

But then, she came.

She came and stole it from him.

And he went closer to where she was, and she did not throw it at him.

* * * * *

Kay Young returned to woozy consciousness to find that she was lying on a soft sofa beneath a heap of quilts near a cheerfully burning fire. When she tried to move, however, everything hurt, and she groaned.

At once she heard a sound, then a stranger with a hard, harsh face was squatting beside her. "Shh," he said softly. "You're safe here. I promise."

"I have to go," she said weakly, struggling against pain. "He'll find me. He can't find me."

"Easy, lady," he said quietly. "You're hurt. No one's going to find you here."

"He will," she said desperately, terror clutching at her insides. "He always finds me!"

"Easy," he said again. "There's a blizzard outside. No one's getting here tonight, not even the doctor. I know, because I tried."

"Doctor? I don't need a doctor! I've got to get away."

"There's nowhere to go tonight," he said levelly. "And if I thought you could stand, I'd take you to a window and show you."

But even as she tried once more to pull away the quilts,

she remembered something else: this man had been gentle when he'd found her beside the road, even when she had kicked and clawed. He hadn't hurt her.

Terror receded just a bit. She looked at him and detected signs of true concern there.

The terror eased another notch and she let her head sag on the pillow. "He always finds me," she whispered.

"Not here. Not tonight. That much I can guarantee."

Will Kay's mysterious rescuer protect her
from her worst fears?
Find out in HER HERO IN HIDING by
New York Times *bestselling author Rachel Lee.*
Available June 2010, only from
Silhouette® Romantic Suspense.

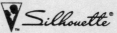
Silhouette®

ROMANTIC
SUSPENSE

Sparked by Danger, Fueled by Passion.

NEW YORK TIMES AND *USA TODAY*
BESTSELLING AUTHOR

RACHEL LEE

BRINGS YOU AN ALL-NEW
CONARD COUNTY: THE NEXT GENERATION SAGA!

After finding the injured Kay Young on a deserted country
road Clint Ardmore learns that she is not only being hunted
by a serial killer, but is also three months pregnant.
He is determined to protect them—even if it means
forgoing the solitude that he has come to appreciate.
But will Clint grow fond of having an attractive woman
occupy his otherwise empty ranch?

Find out in

Her Hero in Hiding

Available June 2010 wherever books are sold.

Visit Silhouette Books at www.eHarlequin.com

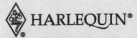

HARLEQUIN®

American ★ Romance®

The Best Man in Texas
TANYA MICHAELS

Brooke Nichols—soon to be Brooke Baker—
hates surprises. Growing up in an unstable
environment, she's happy to be putting down
roots with her safe, steady fiancé. Then she meets
his best friend, Jake McBride, a firefighter and
former soldier who's raw, unpredictable and
passionate. With his spontaneous streak and
dangerous career, Jake is everything Brooke is
trying to avoid…so why is it so hard to resist him?

**Available June
wherever books are sold.**

"LOVE, HOME & HAPPINESS"

www.eHarlequin.com

HAR75315

HARLEQUIN® Romance®

GIRLS' Weekend in VEGAS

Four friends, four dream weddings!

On a girly weekend in Las Vegas, best friends Alex, Molly, Serena and Jayne are supposed to just have fun and forget men, but they end up meeting their perfect matches! Will the love they find in Vegas stay in Vegas?

Find out in this sassy, fun and wildly romantic miniseries all about love and friendship!

Saving Cinderella! by MYRNA MACKENZIE
Available June

Vegas Pregnancy Surprise by SHIRLEY JUMP
Available July

Inconveniently Wed! by JACKIE BRAUN
Available August

Wedding Date with the Best Man
by MELISSA MCCLONE
Available September

www.eHarlequin.com

HR17663